United Trace

L. M. PERALTA

Books by L. M. Peralta

THE ELEMENTALS TRILOGY

The Elementals
The Council
The Creator

THE ARCADIAN STEEL SEQUENCE

The Wings of Heaven and Hell
The Seven Archangels of Heaven
The Seven Princes of Hell

This is a work of fiction. All the characters, organizations, and events portrayed in this book are either products of the author's imagination or are used fictitiously.

UNITED TRACE

First Paperback Edition: September 2016

ISBN: 978-0-9888448-6-5

To Dad.

Because you were the first person
to pick up this book fifteen years ago.

1

Dalton Anderson wasn't an orphan, but he didn't have parents. He never did. From the moment he was born, it wasn't a mother's arms he rested in, but on the belt of an assembly line where he was fed, dressed, and sent off to live in the Community House.

None of the children who lived in the Community House had fathers or mothers. Many were orphans, true orphans who had lost their parents, but not Dalton. He was birthed from an artificial womb. He was part of an experiment to keep the city's population stable. Pollution made it difficult for women to bare children, but in UT City Z3T, they were the last trace of humanity. They had to survive.

Survival. *I hope I survive this*, Dalton thought.

Dalton had braved the Slope before, but never against Jareth. Were the stories about him true? Did a guy die on this thing because of him?

Dalton looked over at Jareth perched on his hoverboard. Dalton couldn't see Jareth's face behind his gas mask.

Dalton's job cleaning the city filters required him to be abled-bodied. He hoped Jareth wouldn't compromise that.

Removing his hoverboard from his back, Dalton placed it on the ground at his feet and stepped on. Dalton's hoverboard was light and thin. He had designed it that way. The light weight of the board made it faster. Its long metallic edge gleamed even in the dim light, but the hoverboard was not beautiful by any stretch of the imagination. The patchwork metal parts were of different colors and textures. He could have painted it to make it more uniform, but that would have added to the weight. With his back foot, Dalton hit the button at the end of the hoverboard, and the board jumped to life. It hovered above the ground next to Jareth's.

The city's dome ceiling loomed above them. The steel-reinforced concrete was vaguely visible through the pollution clouds. The concrete was made with less water than usual and with only the very finest silica sand as its aggregate, making it resistant against explosives. The real secret was a series of narrow, short steel fibers used to reinforce the concrete, making it one hundred times stronger than normal concrete. The large concrete dome encased the city in its protective walls.

The bright florescent lights beaming through the pollution cloud gave the city an overcast, foggy atmosphere.

More miles stretched below than above them. Ayden and Giana looked like ants to Dalton. He could just make out their tiny forms. They said they would be waiting for him at the finish line in the glass encased airlock.

Hopefully they won't have to pick up the pieces, Dalton thought.

Hoverboard racing was the only thing of which Dalton was prideful. His job was just a job. He lived in UT Sector 6 so his apartment wasn't anything to brag about. He learned early on if you don't have parents to celebrate you, you better start celebrating yourself or no one else will.

Focus.

Dalton's eyes focused on the space a few feet in front of him—the Slope's starting line. The Slope was a mess of tubes made of parts of discarded Safe Ways. It spiraled all the way to the ground in a series of twists and turns that would make a normal person sick, but Dalton's stomach was never unsettled by such things. He used to think it was because he had so much practice on the hoverboard, but then again, he could never remember a time it made him sick, not even in the beginning.

Out of the corner of his eye, Dalton saw the white flag wave. In seconds, his foot jabbed the back button on his hoverboard, and he zoomed forward.

The walls of the Slope were all around him. It was like being in a long, wide tunnel made of steel and glass. The glass upper parts of the Safe Way served as windows so people could see the concrete ceiling and the tops of the city buildings. But on the Slope, the glass enclosures were positioned at the bottom of the long tube. This way Dalton could see below him. He could see how far from the ground he was. It also gave the spectators a good view of the race as did the cameras mounted in strategic places along the interior walls of the Slope.

The steel paneling made the floor flat and easy to walk on. That paneling was ripped out of the Slope, leaving only the rounded steel above Dalton's head.

Dalton had the acute sense that Jareth was near him, but he tried not to focus on him. The series of turns were more complicated at the top of the Slope. Dalton curved his hoverboard to the left, then the right.

Jareth laughed as he zoomed ahead.

He's just trying to psych me out, Dalton thought.

It wasn't just about the rider. It was about how well you could craft your hoverboard. Dalton had worked painstakingly on his hoverboard, making it as flat as he could to increase the speed, giving it more turn sensitivity, and increasing its boost capacity. It wasn't the nicest looking hoverboard, but it was powerful.

Dalton tapped the front switch to up his speed.

He was close to Jareth. The wind ripped through his clothes as he passed him.

Just a few more yards, thought Dalton.

Slam!

Jareth's hoverboard smashed into Dalton's. Dalton lost his balance. His gloved hands skid across the steel sides of the Slope. He was going so fast, if it wasn't for his gloves, his hands would have been on fire.

Dalton bounced off the wall and found his balance.

He looked through his gas mask. *Where is he?*

Dalton tapped the switch on the front of the board, upping it to maximum speed. Most riders couldn't control a hoverboard at top speed, especially taking on an obstacle like the Slope.

Dalton curved as he came rushing towards the wall. Another sharp turn followed up ahead. He bent his knees and cleared it.

Jareth turned his head as Dalton neared him. He was zigzagging to prevent Dalton from passing him.

Going maximum speed, and given little time to think, Dalton tilted his hoverboard to the left. He rode up the wall and over Jareth's head before coming down. It all happened in a split second, and he was in front of Jareth.

Dalton came zooming past the finish line. In front of him was a pile of discarded Safe Way steel going all the way to the ceiling. If he didn't stop, he would crash into the pile.

Dalton gritted his teeth. He pushed the hoverboard to the side, his feet now pointing toward the shortest side of the board. He considered sacrificing his board and jumping off, but he had worked so hard on it.

The hoverboard slammed to a halt.

Dalton was jolted from it and onto the ground. The air left his lungs.

Jareth's hoverboard buzzed, coming out of the long, twisting steel and glass tube.

Jareth looked down at him. Dalton knew that he wanted to say something, but it would be unintelligible behind his gas mask.

He walked away from Dalton and into the airlock.

Dalton picked up his hoverboard and approached the glass enclosure. Giana had her fingers pressed to the glass, and Ayden was soundlessly cheering, pumping his fists into the air, and mouthing the words, "What, What!"

Dalton pushed the button to enter the airlock. The door behind him closed securely before the door in front of him opened. Dalton removed his gas mask. He ran his hand through his matted, dark hair.

"Man, you *killed* it." Ayden approached him with his hand in the air, high-fiving his friend. "I've seen some hoverboard racing, and that was the finest I've ever *seen*. Man, the way you went above Jareth's head like that."

The television in the glass enclosed airlock was replaying the moment when Dalton sped over Jareth's head.

Jareth stood in the corner and wiped the filters on the sides of his mask. The spikes in his jet-black hair were flattened from wearing the mask. The bands of tattoos on his arms went all the way down to his wrists. His friends, or rather his goons, stood around him. Their mouths were moving, but Jareth was staring at Dalton.

Dalton tore his eyes away from him.

A girl stood in front of him. Her blonde hair braided. Her eyes somewhat glassy.

"Hey."

"Hey, stranger," said Giana.

"I'm glad you came," said Dalton.

She hugged him awkwardly. "I am too."

The smell of the shampoo in her hair lingered after her touch was gone. It smelled sickly sweet, but he missed it.

She wore that tight, silver dress that Dalton had said he liked. He only said that because it showed off her legs.

Jareth and his friends snickered as they passed. "Test-Tube Baby," one of them said. Dalton wasn't sure which one had said it. It might have been Jareth.

Though Dalton passed all his competency tests by the age of fifteen, his status as a test-tube baby, a laboratory experiment, precluded him from most employment. His access card, which was coded with his identification number, showed his birth status as artificial. This status was designated by the extra string of numbers—596.

Most with Dalton's status were born with birth defects, usually affecting their intelligence, sometimes giving them horrifying physical deformities. That is probably why the experiments stopped shortly after Dalton was born.

Before he left the airlock, Jareth winked at Giana. Dalton was surprised that it *didn't* make his blood boil.

"Don't listen to him," said Giana.

Her advice, her attempt at comfort, seemed forced to Dalton, like she was acting an exaggerated part in a comedy production.

"Man, he's just sore because you knocked him on his ass," said Ayden.

"Actually, I knocked myself on my own ass." Dalton wiped down the filter on the front of his mask.

"You should wear an air tank," said Giana.

"Nah," said Dalton. "It would slow me down. No one wears an air tank in hoverboard racing."

Giana didn't often come to the races. In the first few weeks of their relationship, she had come and cheered him on. He was so excited to be with her, he hadn't noticed how fake it was. After those first few weeks, she stopped coming to the races. Then, in the first few months, she started getting angry at him for going.

"You should want to hang out with me instead," she had said. "You're going to get yourself killed out there."

She doesn't really care if I get myself killed, Dalton had thought.

Dalton shook his head. Of course, she cared, she was my girlfriend.

He had met Giana on the Air Shuttle. The Shuttle was crowded so she took a seat next to his.

"So, where do you go to school?" she asked.

It surprised him. Normally, people kept to themselves when sitting next to strangers on the Air Shuttle, especially girls, but not Giana.

There were two schools in UT City Z3T, a private school and a public school. From her uniform, Dalton could tell she went to the fancy private school.

Dalton had gone to the public school, but he was out of there now so he didn't have to admit that. Both schools had day and night classes, so his lack of uniform wouldn't be all too telling anyway.

"I completed my competency tests." Dalton turned his head, but didn't make direct eye contact with her.

"Your competency tests? How old are you?"

"Sixteen."

"Whoa."

Dalton didn't tell her he worked in air filter clean-up. He hoped that wouldn't be her next question. He shuffled in his seat, trying to think of something he could ask her before it got to that.

Her uniform was purple that meant she was in Secondary School, which also meant she would be two maybe three years older than Dalton.

"Um . . . where do you go to school?" he asked.

Giana tapped the embroidered badge on her school uniform. "UTC Academy." The badge depicted the sun with pointed rays radiating out from its round center. Under the emblem was a banner with UTCA stitched in.

Dalton wondered if the sun really looked like that.

He looked up at her. She was pretty, probably the prettiest girl he'd ever seen.

From then on, Giana sat next to him as he left for work on the Shuttle. He let her do most of the talking. She liked to talk about herself . . . a lot. It made it easier to keep certain aspects of his life secret from her, like his job and his apartment in the worse sector of the city.

Dalton boarded the Air Shuttle with Giana and Ayden.

He sat at a window seat. Ayden moved to sit next to him when a loud, "Ahem," issued forth.

Giana was behind Ayden.

"Oh," Ayden said. "Sorry." He moved aside to let Giana sit next to Dalton. Ayden sat in the row in front of theirs.

Ayden turned around in his seat. "Man, do you think Jareth will send his goons to beat you up? You did hurt his pride and all."

"I wouldn't put it past him." Dalton wanted to say, *I'd like to see him try.* But he held back. *It's her*, he thought. *I'm still trying to impress her.* He wondered if Ayden could tell. He probably could. They had been friends for ten years.

"They're a bunch of idiots," said Giana.

Something about her joining in on a conversation involving Jareth was unsettling to Dalton. But, after all, she should know more about Jareth than either of them.

Dalton watched the images blur outside the window. He wanted to get off the Shuttle. He didn't care if Giana finally discovered that he lived in UT Sector 6. He just wanted to escape the uncomfortable silences and his inability to be real with Ayden when she was around.

Even being around Ayden was making him uncomfortable. He knew his friend was probably judging him. This girl broke his heart in the worse way, and Dalton wasn't saying anything about it. In fact, he was trying to *impress* her by being what she wanted him to be: intelligent, composed, and submissive to the extreme. She wanted the perfect guy, but she also wanted him to know that *she* was better than him.

It isn't that obvious, is it? Dalton continued to look out the window. Maybe I'm being paranoid.

The Shuttle stopped at Sector 9. Ayden got up from his seat and shouldered his backpack. "See ya tomorrow, man." Ayden's eyelids drooped, and he did not make eye contact with Dalton. The corners of his lips were down-turned, like he was leaving his friend outside without a gas mask.

Dalton watched Ayden get off at Sector 9. His palms were starting to sweat. He heard the doors close. He could sense Giana's presence beside him much more acutely than before.

Should I say something to her? What would I say to her? "Ayden's nice."

What was she playing at? She never liked Ayden.

"Sure." Dalton shifted in his seat.

"That was brave what you did out there," she said.

He swallowed. "I thought you didn't like the racing."

"Well, it's dangerous," she said. "But if you like it that much."

You're a bad actress, he thought. Giana was never wrong, and she *never* changed her mind.

Silence hung in the air. Out of the corner of his eye, Dalton could see Giana's fingers interlocking. Then, her hands smoothed out her already perfectly laid skirt before coming to rest in her lap.

"I missed you," she said, suddenly.

Dalton didn't say anything.

Giana's hands clasped and unclasped. "I want us to get back together."

* * *

Dalton threw his access card on the counter and sauntered over to his couch. He slumped down on the couch and grabbed the remote. He flipped through the channels. He found a late-night talk show he had heard of but never watched before.

The flattened holograph image of the talk show host wavered in the air above the long, metal box. Dalton had tried to fix it himself, but televisions were very different from hoverboards. When it first started, the wavering images made him sick, but now he was used to it.

He could bring it in for repairs, but the embarrassment of having such an outdated device would weigh on him. He had pulled it out of someone else's trash.

Besides, the money could be spent on more important things, like a new apartment filter. The fibers on his were becoming worn and having an outdated air filter could land you in the hospital for a couple days on breathing treatments. That would cost more than the filters themselves on missed work hours alone.

He peeled off his gloves and threw them beside the television. He discarded his shirt into the pile of dirty clothes in the corner of the room.

He laid out on the couch and ignored the drone of the talk show in the background. A cockroach scurried down the wall. He was too tired to kill it. He hoped he didn't find it in his breakfast the next morning.

He shifted on the couch. His ass still hurt from when he hit the ground. It felt bruised, and the cheap couch wasn't helping. Dalton looked around his one bedroom apartment. There were a couple of pillows tossed into the corner of the room, but he wasn't going to get up to get them, not unless he got restless.

He turned over onto his stomach. His neck would hurt in the morning, but at least he'd be able to get to sleep.

Giana. Dalton sighed. He hated that he had to think about her. He had let her go, wiped his hands of her, and stopped thinking about her.

Now, all he could think about were her soft hands as she clasped and unclasped them in her lap, of the smell of her sickly-sweet shampoo, and the false promises she made.

It wasn't easy being with her, but that was just how girls were.

She hadn't asked *him* what *he* wanted. She stated that she wanted them to get back together, like what he had to say about it really didn't matter. She assumed that he wanted her back. And he did.

She was controlling and stifling, but what was his alternative? Some girl, some new stranger he would have to get to know, who might even be worse?

It was crazy but . . . he *did* want her back.

2

"I'm sorry, man." Ayden jabbed his finger down on the X button, making his player jump towards Dalton's player.

Dalton defended his kick, backing away from Ayden's player, but his mind was elsewhere, and his friend wasn't helping.

"I mean . . . she just showed up. I didn't know what to say to her."

"I didn't know she showed up for me." One corner of Dalton's lips tightened. "Look, can we stop talking about it now. I'm really trying to get my mind off the whole thing."

"Sure." Ayden's player brought his fists down to hit the ground. A quake rippled, knocking Dalton's player off his feet.

"Pwned!" Ayden flicked his hand up into the air.

The holograph characters fizzled in and out of focus. Ayden's player was crouching and standing in a loop.

"Shit! It glitched again." Ayden was just about to reset the Xeclade, when Derek came into the room and grabbed the remote.

"Alright, it's time to get off this shit, boys." Derek changed the channel to a news broadcast station.

"Hey, man. Turn it back." Ayden tried to grab the remote from his brother, but Derek held it up in the air out of Ayden's reach. He leaned one arm on the back of the sofa.

A hologram image of the news reporter spoke. "It's the latest standard issue," she said, with an unnatural inflection in her voice. Hologram images of the new model of air filtration system appeared. "They are designed to keep our homes safer and make breathing easier."

"You'll be breathing easier, Leanne." The male news reporter turned to her.

"Yes, Paul. My new filtration system was just installed, and I can't recommend it enough. It's more powerful and requires less cleaning."

They're trying to limit my work hours, thought Dalton. *Good luck*. Less cleaning just meant not cleaning every day, probably still every other day though. Most people would be too scared not to have them cleaned every day anyway. Filter maintenance had the most jobs of any industry in UTC.

"Man, you put on some boring crap." Ayden folded his arms.

"Shut it," said Derek. "This is it."

Leanne's face was front and center again. "Eskov Energy has just announced its newest Systems Director. Derek Haley will be filling the position after a lengthy internal recruitment process. Eskov Energy will also be making improvements to the MCG, the city's most powerful generator."

Images of the MCG appeared coupled with images of the outside of Eskov Energy's main building, the largest building in UTC. The sprawling buildings surrounding it were abandoned. The filters were out of date, and the buildings were improperly sealed. One inhale of the outside air could send a young person to the hospital for a few days with frequent breathing treatments. It could kill an older person. The ashes would be burned, sending more pollution into the air.

Dalton's eyes drifted to Leanne's chest. She wore a low-cut shirt that went down with a "V" plunge into her cleavage. Suddenly, the television blinked off.

"What do you think?" Derek threw the remote between Dalton and Ayden on the couch.

Ayden's lips, the corners downturned, went up to his nose. He gave a shrug. "I mean it's great, right? Though they only spent like five seconds on you."

"It's not about popularity," said Derek. "I'm being promoted to one of the top positions in the city. That not only means a bigger paycheck, but I'll also get a seat on the Assembly. I'll get the chance to make a difference."

"What kind of a difference?" Ayden asked.

"Well, for starters," said Derek. "The Safe Ways are constantly needing repair. I could vote to have funding shift to making them safer and more reliable. They put funding into getting a new Mega Screen every year. Why not put that money into the Safe Ways instead?"

"Isn't the Assembly made up of something like a hundred people?" asked Dalton. "People get excited about the Mega Screen and forget their other problems. That's why they upgrade the screen every year. They can watch the Mega Screen from almost anywhere in the city and get lost in it."

"Man," said Ayden, his voice becoming lower. "That's deep. I never thought of it that way."

Derek drummed his fingers on the sofa. He went to the kitchen. The only thing separating the living room from the kitchen was a countertop peninsula. Derek and Ayden's apartment wasn't as small as Dalton's, and it was certainly in a better part of the city. It was roughly double the size, but that wasn't saying all that much. Dalton's apartment only had two rooms, and one was the bathroom. Dalton wondered if Derek and Ayden would move into a nicer Sector to reflect Derek's promotion.

Derek took a beer from the refrigerator and popped the cap off. He took a swig and sat at one of the bar stools lining the peninsula. "Well, I'm going to make my vote count."

No one liked to hear that they didn't matter. Especially not someone like Derek, thought Dalton. I shouldn't have said anything. It didn't make a difference anyway.

"Hey, man, you wanna play?" Ayden had reset the Xeclade.

"Sure." Dalton grabbed the controller.

*   *   *

Dalton had his hands in his pockets and his head down as he marched through the Safe Way to Sector 6. You didn't want to make eye contact with anyone in Sector 6. There were a lot of crazies hanging around. But you still wanted to be on your guard at the same time. With his head down, Dalton could hear a pin drop. It was an easy way to avoid eye contact yet remain alert.

Dalton had lived in Sector 6 for almost two years now. He took his competency tests early so that he could get a job and move out of the Community House. Things had always been competitive there. It would be a battle over food, blankets, clothes, and especially when prospective parents rolled through.

Of course, having parents wasn't something Dalton could hope for. He was labeled a Test-Tube Baby and no one wanted a kid that was grown in a lab, not when they could have a normal healthily functioning child.

He couldn't pack his bags fast enough, and thankfully, he didn't have much to pack. Even two years later, he didn't think he could fill one whole suitcase with his small pile of belongings. Of course, he had saved up enough to buy a busted old couch and went rummaging through the trash to find an out-of-date television, which displayed flatter, more pixelated holographs.

Back in the Community House, it had never been the lack of belongings or nice things that bothered Dalton. After all, he didn't have much now either. It was the constant competition, the controversy, and the fighting.

Coupled with all that, he hated when volunteers came to talk to him about his feelings, his habits, or his dreams. *Counseling.* How could someone who had never been through what he had been through, who had parents, ever help him with his problems? He would have rather them come to talk about how he could get out sooner.

Music played from the sound system in the Safe Way. That meant the latest music video from Caustic Embers was playing on the Mega Screen.

Someone brushed past Dalton.

". . . The city's bad air . . . it's getting *in*. Beyond the wall, they're hiding heaps and heaps of trash like towers. Soon, we'll be swimming in our own discarded waste. Updating the filters, sealing the Safe Ways, tossing chemicals in the water to *clean* it . . . putting blinders on us while the city goes to hell. They should be trying to get us out."

The voice was becoming louder until Dalton sensed hands reaching for him. He backed away just in time.

It was a man. His face and clothes were dirty as if he had been swimming in the crap he was preaching against. His eyes darted like he was blind, and when he focused on him, Dalton wasn't sure if he could see him.

The music of Caustic Embers was all background now. In fact, Dalton couldn't hear anything else around him.

"How many times can we recycle our own shit?"

It was as if Dalton had blinders on, and all he could see was this dirty, old man. Then, into the frame came hands that grabbed the man about the shoulders. A cop was pulling him away, removing him from the Safe Way.

It was as if the man rose from the trash piles to warn them, only to be tossed back beyond the walls, where he would be tucked away so the people of UTC wouldn't have to think their city was going to shit.

Dalton glanced up at the monitor. Monitors lined the Safe Way. The monitors never bothered Dalton before, but he suddenly got the feeling he was being watched.

3

Dalton put on his hazmat suit and shouldered his air tank. He walked along the hallway of Sector 11, the waste management sector.

A man with a tablet walked past him and swung open the door to the water filtration plant.

Dalton had never seen what went on in the filtration plant. He had never been curious enough to check it out. But, the old man's words echoed in his mind: *How many times can we recycle our own shit?*

Dalton slinked past the swinging door and into the treatment facility.

Huge clear vats were filled with liquid waste funneling in from large sewage tunnels. Dalton put his arm up to his nose.

The men on the galley ways above the vats wore masks that covered their mouths and noses.

I thought my job was bad.

The watery waste was channeled through large filters that separated the larger debris from the liquid. Dalton knew where this was going, but he dared not call it water. He knew that the water had been reused for probably hundreds of years, but he still didn't like to think about it.

He looked down to the end of the assembly line. Different colored chemicals were mixed into the liquid to kill any remaining bacteria before it was sent back up the pipes.

Dalton wished he had a better home filtration system, but he doubted that would quell his disgust.

"Hey, what are you doing in here?" A voice came from the galley way.

Dalton didn't look up when he heard the voice. He hastened for the door and left the filtration plant behind him, wishing he hadn't gone in there in the first place.

* * *

"Hey, Dalton." It was Ingrid. She had on her hazmat suit. "You're early. What were you doing in there?"

Ingrid had her long hair tied up in a bun. She had an ashy smudge on her chin that Dalton didn't tell her about. She wasn't pretty anyway.

"Nothing." Dalton shook his head. "I caught the early Shuttle."

He took the early Shuttle because he wanted to avoid
Giana. She took evening classes, so she usually took the shuttle
home right as Dalton was coming into work. He had said that
he needed time, but as soon as she saw him again, she would
expect an answer.

Ingrid put her gas mask on and connected it to her air tank.
The microphone inside the mask made it easy for her to
communicate with him even though the mask covered her
mouth. "Let's get to work." Her tone was what passed for
enthusiasm.

Dalton put on his mask and walked alongside Ingrid.

"How's your mom doing?" he asked.

"Better," she said. "The doctors say she's gonna be fine. She
was in the hospital for five weeks on breathing treatments every
three hours. I'm still nervous about it."

"Did they fix the air leak?"

"They resealed the entire apartment. Cost a fortune, but
they used that new sealant, so it's supposed to last forever."

They'll have a new one out next month. "So, are you gonna get
the stuff?" he asked.

"For *my* apartment? You know I can't afford that . . . not
with this job. And I can't get a new one because I can't pass the
competencies."

I passed my competency tests, thought Dalton. And I'm still
stuck with this shit job. Well, not quite as much shit as they're
dealing with in water filtration. I guess that's how it goes
though: more shit, less risk.

"I'm cutting my life in half at this job," said Ingrid. "But what choice do I have?"

"You could pass your competencies." It didn't sound as harsh because no one he worked with knew Dalton had passed his competencies. He liked it better that way because had they known he passed, they would start wondering why he was stuck cleaning city filters. They might come to realize he was a Test-Tube Baby.

He had shared that one intimate fact with Giana, and she had shared it with Jareth.

"Pass my competencies?" Ingrid swiped her access card over the airlock's security screen. "That's easier said than done."

The airlock hissed as the pressure was released. Dalton stepped through the first door with Ingrid, and she closed it behind them. She pressed the button to the second door, and the same hiss greeted them before they exited into the open air of the city.

The dark air drifted around the buildings. The ground disappeared beneath the dark cloud. The air seemed alive the way it twisted and turned around corners. The lights of the Sectors couldn't be seen through the murkiness of the air.

Dalton pressed the switch on the side of his gas mask, and his flashlight came on. The light cut through the air.

The door opened behind them, and the rest of the team flooded out.

Felix clapped Dalton on the shoulder. "You ready to work, son." The way Felix always called him "son" endeared him to the old man. It gave him a sense of belonging. Dalton considered getting a fake access card that didn't have an extra string of numbers, designating him as an artificial birth, but then he would have to leave this "family." Fake access cards were risky business anyway.

"We have a rookie today," said Felix. "I hope he can learn from you."

Dalton could tell the rookie was skinny even in his hazmat suit. He couldn't be a kid. Teenagers and younger adults usually got jobs working at food departments and restaurants where the hours were more flexible and the money wasn't good enough to live on. They were typically studying for their competencies which most people didn't take until they were twenty-five. So, this guy was either in the exact same situation as Dalton or he had failed his competencies. It was unlikely that he shared the same background as Dalton. Dalton might have been the only successful outcome that came from the artificial birth trials. Most Test-Tube Babies weren't running on a full tank.

"This is Glenn." Felix threw Glenn a wire brush.

* * *

Felix turned off Tower 8 so the air would stop funneling in from the tower. The Tower could only be offline for a couple hours, just long enough for them to clean the filters and move on to the next one.

Dalton was on the lift with Felix, Glenn, and Randolph, who everyone just called Ran-Ran. Dalton wasn't sure if the name meant anything. He started working two years ago, and

Ran-Ran and the crew had been working together years before then. Dalton assumed they called him Ran-Ran because no one on the crew wanted to say Randolph.

The lift took them all the way to the top of the tower. Dalton and Ran-Ran unscrewed the venting and placed it against the side of the tower. Inside were several closely packed filters, all dark with debris.

What was strange about Tower 8 was that no one knew where it filtered the air to, not even the men who cleaned it. All the other filter towers had been accounted for, but not Tower 8.

Dalton took out the first filter and wiped it down, cleaning it in long, efficient strokes.

A dark cloud passed his eyes.

"No, you're doing it wrong." Felix grabbed the filter Glenn had been holding. "You have to make long horizontal wipes, boy. Not that vertical back and forth movement you do with your hand under the sheets."

Ran-Ran laughed. "You're just worried, old man. Worried he'll replace you."

"Replace me?" Felix started wiping down his filter. "I'll die long before any of ya could replace me. I've breathed in enough of this stuff."

Felix was hinting at how woefully ineffective their breathing masks were. It was true, Felix was lucky, most men on the job didn't live within a decade of how long he had been ticking. He figured the clock would stop for him any day now.

Dalton remembered his first day on the job. His muscles were so sore the following morning. Now, he was used to the work. He doubted the skinny man would stay skinny for long.

He figured Felix felt good about correcting the younger man. It made him feel like his job required a degree of skill. Felix's eye was fastened upon Dalton on his first day, but Dalton never gave him a reason to correct him.

It was easy to accept Dalton as smarter than most than to admit the job just didn't require that steep of a learning curve.

Tower 8 was now enveloped in a thick cloud. Dalton couldn't see beyond the churning debris even with his flashlight. Once they were finished with the last of the filters, Dalton helped the others stack them back into the tower. They replaced the vent and then, moved onto the vent right below them.

They cleaned three more towers that night. The morning crew would handle four more, and then the afternoon and evening crews would get to the rest.

Dalton liked working with the night crew. He didn't have to march down crowded Safe Ways on his way home, and the Air Shuttle was practically empty as well. It afforded him plenty of time to think.

As they walked back to the airlock, Dalton took up the rear of the company. He watched the backs of the crew as their flashlights pointed into the distance. There was someone missing—the new guy.

Dalton looked around.

There he was, kneeling beside some debris. Dalton could just barely make out his small form crouched among the pollution leaden air settling close to the ground.

"Hey . . . um, Glenn?" Dalton's microphone was going in and out. He hit the side of his gas mask. "Hey!" The microphone was out.

The rest of the crew had moved on. Dalton could no longer see their forms in the distance.

As much as he didn't want to walk off the road after a long night's shift, he sauntered over to where Glenn was kneeling.

"Hey, man." The mask muffled his voice. But before he could get close enough to touch Glenn, the ground gave out from under him.

Dalton reached up instinctively, trying to grab a hold of anything that might save him, but he found nothing to grab onto. Dalton hit onto deeper ground. He was in a tunnel with what looked like concrete siding. He squinted.

A light glowed at the end of the tunnel, not like a flashlight . . . brighter. *Where's that coming from?*

The ground caved into the tunnel, sending broken cement down. Dalton scrambled out of the way just in time, but his air tank scraped the concrete beneath him. As he sat up, he heard a loud hiss. He was propelled from where he sat as the oxygen was released from his tank in a loud hissing death call. His head hit something with a clang. And then . . . darkness.

4

Dalton blinked.

The debris that had caved in on him blocked the tunnel from where he had seen the strange light emitting.

He reached for the back of his head. It throbbed. He hit something metal. He turned and looked up. It was a ladder.

The tunnel curved upwards, and the ladder ran up this vertical turn into darkness. Dalton couldn't remember if there should be a building above him. He had been thrown several yards from where he originally fell.

Air was still hissing out of his tank.

Shit!

Dalton reached into the tackle bag attached to his side, and grabbed the tape. He cut the tape with his teeth and patched his air tank. He couldn't hear the hissing anymore.

He sighed.

He was sitting in water, four or five inches deep and along the entire length of the tunnel. The water was murky and thick.

The tunnel continued past the ladder and faded into darkness. He wondered if he could reach ground level by climbing the ladder instead of having to climb the cement debris that had fallen into the tunnel.

He reached around and grabbed one side of the ladder and pulled himself up to a standing position. Taking the rigs one step at a time, soon he was nearing the top of the ladder. Dalton pulled himself up onto the landing.

In front of him was a door made of metal like an airlock. There weren't any switches on the wall and no other way to open it. There was, however, a small dirty window at the top of the door.

Dalton tried his best to wipe it clean with the elbow of his hazmat suit. It wasn't an entirely successful attempt, but he could see into the window more clearly.

Behind the door was a large room, completely white. The room sat below the door, like you would have to descend another ladder down into the room. There were rows and rows of white tables. There were microscopes and cages alongside the wall. *An underground . . . lab?*

A man in a lab coat walked in, and Dalton ducked away from the window. He rushed down the ladder and jumped to the floor with only a few rigs remaining. The dirty water splashed around him.

Dalton climbed the debris up to the surface where he had fallen. Some of the cement stones were loose and rolled when his feet landed on them. Dalton struggled to keep his balance. He grabbed the rusty, jagged edge of the tunnel, trying to pull himself up. It bit into his gloved hand. Blood dripped down onto his hazmat suit.

A hand reached out to him.

Dalton grabbed it, and strong arms pulled him back up. He felt more hands grip his hazmat suit and the arm of his bloodied hand.

It was Felix and his crew.

Once Dalton was on safer ground, Felix grabbed Dalton's cut hand. "Oh, that looks bad, my boy."

"Was that guy, Glenn, with you?" asked Ingrid.

"No," said Dalton. "I thought I saw him crouched close to where I fell." His voice was muffled because his microphone had failed.

"Crouched?" she asked.

"Yeah." Dalton held up his bloodied hand. He heard that was good to do. "Crouched in the debris."

"Creepy," said Ran-Ran.

"That cut don't look good," said Felix. "You shouldn't be out here with it. Ingrid, take the boy back to Sector 11. The rest of the crew and I will look for that little creep."

Ingrid and Dalton walked back to the airlock. Blood dripped onto the floor as they marched down the hallway. The cut was deep. Dalton could see the full magnitude of it now that they were under the bright, florescent lights of Sector 11. He pooled the blood into his palm to keep it off the floor.

Ingrid took Dalton's hand and put it over the large sink. The water pressure was too hard and Dalton yanked his hand from under the stream.

"Oh, sorry." Ingrid lowered the water pressure.

The water ran over Dalton's hand and commingled with the blood.

"Take the glove off," said Ingrid.

Dalton pulled the glove from his hand and tossed it to the bottom of the sink.

"Here, let me help you with this." Ingrid disconnected his mask from the air tank and slipped the mask over his head.

Dalton's face was sweaty, and the sweat dripped down, mixing with the blood and water in the sink.

"Looks like you damaged your tank." Ingrid helped him take it off. "We should probably put some disinfectant on it." Ingrid took off her mask and tank and discarded them on the bench in the changing room. She took the safety kit off the wall and found the disinfectant. It was in a small squeeze bottle. She removed the cap and turned the running water off.

"Ok," she said. "I think this is where I should say *this is probably gonna hurt*." She squeezed the bottle, and clear disinfectant solution jetted onto Dalton's hand.

He cringed. "Ah!" He let the solution sting his hand though he got the urge to run it under the water again.

Ingrid took out the bandages and looked down at his hand. "You might need some stitches."

"You gonna stitch it up for me?"

"If only I knew how." She bandaged his hand with the gauze. Once she had a thick roll of gauze around his hand, she taped off the end. "That'll have to do for now."

She helped Dalton onto the bench in the changing room. Behind him, she opened her locker and removed her hazmat suit and her clothes beneath.

Dalton could see her reflection in the mirror above the sink. She had a nice body. Curvy and full.

Ingrid covered her nakedness with a towel and headed for the showers. Dalton thought he'd let her finish first before going in himself.

* * *

Dalton toweled his hair before coming out of the showers. He pulled on a t-shirt and sweat pants.

"You should go," said Ingrid, swiping her finger across the tablet to see the next page of the article she had been reading. Her hair was down and wet. "They'll probably search for some time yet. You know how Felix is."

"What about you?"

Ingrid shut down her tablet and put it into her bag. "Already on my way out. Just had to make sure you didn't pass out in the shower from all that blood loss. You should really go to the hospital."

"They'll charge me an arm and a leg," said Dalton. "That's not worth a hand."

"You might get an infection." Ingrid shouldered her bag. "I don't think that safety kit crap can combat the really bad stuff."

"I think I'll survive." He shut his locker. "I think the only really bad stuff lurks in my apartment."

"Now I know you've lost too much blood. I'd better go before you ask me out for a drink."

Dalton wondered if she noticed him checking her out in the mirror.

Her long hair trailing behind her, Ingrid disappeared around the corner.

Dalton pulled on his socks and his shoes, and grabbed the long, broad strap of his duffle bag. The sudden change of equilibrium caused Dalton to take a sharp step forward to regain his balance. He wondered how long the body took to regain its blood supply. He must have lost a few pints at least. His hand was still bleeding through the thick roll of gauze.

* * *

Dalton boarded the Air Shuttle. He sat in the back of the car and laid across two seats. It didn't matter anyway, very few people boarded the Air Shuttle after 2 A.M. Dalton let his mind drift.

Giana would find a way to meet up with him eventually. He couldn't keep ignoring her calls. If he had taken Ingrid out for that drink, he could give Giana the excuse that he's seeing someone else. He shook his head. Many women looked like Ingrid, but very few looked like Giana.

Giana would see right through that.

Dalton felt himself drifting, then the Air Shuttle jerked to a stop. Dalton looked around. The car was empty. A monitor hung from the ceiling at the front of the car. The red light on the monitor read: Sector 6.

Dalton jolted up and grabbed his bag. He marched down the aisle and off the Shuttle. He entered the Safe Way to Sector 6.

Something weird was going on.

The lights in the Safe Way were off. The only thing that lit the long hallway was the glow from the Mega Screen.

But something else was wrong.

Even in the earliest hours of the morning the Mega Screen would blare some late-night talk show or music channel, but the screen was bright orange and wavered in the air. *A malfunction?* Dalton wondered. *They* are *always replacing the thing.*

Footsteps echoed behind him.

Dalton turned around. He looked down the long, wide hallway. There was no one—wait!

Against one side of the hallway, hidden in the shadows, there *was* someone. Dalton could just make out the outline of a figure wearing what he could only assume was an out-of-date gas mask. The masks of the prior decade tended to be bulker and more burdensome. No one wore them anymore, but Dalton remembered them from his early childhood.

The thing in the corner let out a loud breath. It was muffled by the mask, but Dalton could still hear it funneling down the Safe Way.

Why is he wearing a mask in the Safe Way? Dalton wondered.

He didn't want to acknowledge this oddball, so he started walking faster towards his apartment. He rounded the bend and looked out the windows. The Mega Screen was still orange and blinking in and out.

He looked down the hallway he'd just turned into. The thing wasn't following him. He glanced back at the window. The Safe Way wrapped around the apartment building with windows lining the entire length of it. From the window where Dalton was standing, he could see through to the hallway where he had just left.

There, standing right in front of the window in the adjacent hallway, was the thing in the outdated mask. It was staring through the window, right at *him*.

Dalton ran down the Safe Way in the direction of his apartment. Feet thundered behind him. Dalton slid around the corner, almost falling to his knees. He dropped his bag, but he didn't go back for it.

The breathing grew louder. Dalton sensed it was right behind him. He could imagine the long, thin body and lanky arms reaching out to him.

Dalton reached inside his pocket for his access card. He pushed the card into the door slot. He didn't dare to look. Even if he made it by just a hair, it would give him chills to know that, and even if he didn't make it, well, he'd rather cross that bridge if it came to it.

The door buzzed open.

Dalton rushed in and slammed the door shut.

He pushed the metal covering back and peered out the small window at the top of his front door. There was no one in the hallway, at least, not from what he could tell from the limited view the small window gave him.

Dalton sighed and peeled off his shirt.

He piled the pillows on top of his couch and laid down, but he doubted he would get any sleep. He turned on the television, but all he got was orange light. He flicked through the channels: more of the same. He turned the television off, and turned around to face the back of the couch.

* * *

Dalton was running. Running through fields of vegetation and fresh water. He didn't know what he was running from, but he knew he was running from something. He couldn't let it catch him or he would die.

A dazzling light shone from where the concrete ceiling should be, but there was no concrete ceiling, just open . . . air.

It wasn't darkened or dirty, and Dalton wasn't wearing a gas mask or an air tank or a hazmat suit.

The wind brushed his skin. Beads of sweat formed on his brow. He must have run the length of a hundred UT Cities. The light in the sky was a thousand times brighter than the most brilliant fluorescent lights.

X

Hello! I am Urtel Tuvesri. If you understand this transmission that is because the system has detected your language and has translated it to you. I, myself, speak several Earth languages, but as I don't know which one you speak, the language detector will certainly be a great benefit.

I have studied Earth for centuries, your history, your accomplishments, your music. I especially like the works of Bob Dylan.

This is a picture of me and my mothers. They died about fifty years ago.

I thought, maybe, it would be a good idea to introduce myself to you. I guess, partly, I'm also doing this so I won't go crazy.

Ah, it's been roughly twenty years since the others left. Not that I don't have things to entertain me. I have catalogues full of music, books, and movies, but I've learned that having someone to talk to is so important.

I know you're probably thinking that talking to a camera is not the same. Yeah, it's not, but it's something to pass the time.

Besides, you're going to need instructions. And I'll get to that. I have a lot of time. At least another ten years before I go into a *long* sleep.

There's nothing worse than a restless sleep, so I've been doing a lot. Getting exercise, exploring, reading, and watching. But I think sleeping will be good for me. I might get to talk to others in my dreams, then I won't feel so alone.

I'm currently in the middle of one of your movies. I don't know if you've seen it. It's the one where the man dies and lives on in his widow's paintings. I can't remember the name right now. It'll come to me.

You see, where I'm from, the arts aren't really appreciated. That's part of the reason I've always admired humans.

I could spend hours listening to your music.

In my early life stage, I discovered a catalogue full of Earth music. I listened to it all night. My mothers thought something was wrong with me when I didn't come out of my room. They called the doctors who gave me a mood changer. I was able to focus on my studies for a time, but then I found another catalogue and became absorbed in that. Eventually, my mothers stopped calling the doctor.

I guess you could say I was an odd child. I didn't have any friends. A few of my classmates were on the same educational track, but few of them obsessed over any one lifeform. Specialization simply didn't exist. A few of my professors had discussed with my mothers my *unnatural* preoccupation with humans.

I knew it was strange, but it never *felt* strange.

My mothers arranged my union with Ren Tervi once I completed my first century. I told them I didn't love her. They were confused. I learned that word "love" from Earth movies and books.

The doctor gave me a mood changer, but it didn't make me feel love. It made me feel compliance. I know that is not an emotion among humans, but on Wen, we consider it a *feeling*. It removes all else from your mind and makes your decisions more malleable. The only thing is, compliance can only be used a few times before it becomes ineffective, my mothers had used it too often on me.

I refused to unite with Ren Tervi, and she united with another. This is why I have no children. I could have combined my DNA with Ren's, but I couldn't imagine having to unite with her.

My mothers were very disappointed in me. They had been friends with Ren's family for centuries and as all other compatible DNA was united, I ended up without a companion. My mothers seemed to think it was the worst thing in the world.

I didn't care. To this day, I don't care. I would have never obtained a companion that understands me.

She would have called the doctor every time I spoke of humans or Earth. I would have become addicted to mood changers.

I started changing my sleep cycles so I wouldn't run into Ren's family. It is illegal to change one's sleep cycles, but I was willing to undergo the risk. I started sleeping during solar hours even though my apartment was designed to generate red light during those hours.

I'll admit, it was difficult to sleep at first, but I eventually got used to it.

I started to get stares on the street. It was obvious I had designed lunar gear to pass as a lunar walker. Even the color of my skin betrayed me.

But that's all past me now.

I feel this is important that you get to know me, but I guess I should begin at the beginning. After all, I don't want you to be scared.

5

Dalton woke to something tickling his face. He swiped at it. The roach hit the wall and scurried to the corner of the room.

Dalton ran his hand through his hair and yawned.

He couldn't feel his right hand. The bandage was soaked in blood.

Dalton sauntered over to the kitchen and poured himself a bowl of cereal. A cockroach came tumbling out with the cereal.

Dalton swept the bowl off the counter. It landed with a crash at the other end of the room. He smacked his forehead with his hand and sighed. "Alright."

Dalton took off the shirt he wore the night before and pulled on a fresh one. Grabbing a pair of pants from the floor, he struggled to put them on with one hand.

He didn't have any fresh gauze so he donned his hoverboard racing gloves. He had some trouble getting the tight-fitting glove over the thick layers of gauze.

He grabbed his access card from the counter and left the apartment.

People were walking through the Safe Way with bags like they had just come back from a vacation in Sector 15.

Dalton raised his eyebrow.

Mrs. Cindergard, his neighbor, was carrying an overnight bag and had her gas mask on, but Dalton could tell it was her from the silver scarf she always wore when she went out.

Dalton waved to her slowly as she passed. He walked down the Safe Way and turned to look as Mrs. Cindergard put her access card into her door slot.

Dalton saw his bag. He remembered he dropped it last night as he ran from that guy in the Safe Way. He picked it up and walked back to his apartment. He put his access card into the slot and threw his bag inside. He didn't see where it had landed, but he didn't care.

He made it through the crowd on the Safe Way and called Ayden to meet him in Sector 14 for lunch. The Mega Screen was operating fine that morning. A large image of the news anchor Leanne was suspended in the air. She was saying something about UTC's latest fashion trends. Dalton wasn't listening.

He ambled onto the Air Shuttle. Giana sat a few rows from the front. She was looking down at her holo-screen. He knew he would run into her sooner or later. He pretended he hadn't seen her, but no one could ignore her bright blonde hair. He thought she might have the only true blonde hair in the city.

Dalton diverted his eyes and turned his head away from Giana. He took a seat in the back of the Air Shuttle and put the headphones on.

The dream he had the night before entered his mind. The memory of it was starting to fade, but he did remember one thing quite vividly: the bright light in the open air.

There was a song about that by the Caustic Embers. It was back when they weren't really anything. Dalton was at a club in Sector 16, and they were playing. It was before he met Giana.

He didn't have any money, and Ayden thought it would be cool if they met some girls there. Dalton didn't really care. He just wanted to get out of his apartment.

He was at the bar when the band started playing a song that really got to him. It mentioned the open air and "the Sun." They described it as a bright light in the sky, bright enough to light the whole city and beyond. Dalton didn't know what they had meant by "beyond." *To the trash heaps beyond the city walls?*

Dalton had what he thought was a pretty good concept of what the Sun was. He had remembered studying it. It was part of what the world used to be before the catastrophe.

Dalton heard that the song was banned. The word was that it had been too racy. It *did* juxtapose images of sex and fondling with a feeling like they had seen *the Sun.*

Shortly after word got out that the song was banned, the Caustic Embers started being featured on the Mega Screen. Of course, their songs were cleaner, not the type that you would hear in some seedy bar.

Someone sat in the seat beside him. It was Giana.

Her perfume wafted up his nostrils. It smelled fruity, but it was a fruit Dalton couldn't name.

He took off the headphones.

"You didn't answer my calls." She wore a tight bodysuit, which Dalton thought he might have seen when he glanced up at the Mega Screen that morning. It showed off Giana's figure, which made it hard not to stare at her.

"I dropped my access card," said Dalton. "Now, it won't display calls or texts."

Dalton knew she wanted to say, *"Let me see your access card!"* But she bit her lip.

She turned her legs towards him. "So . . . I gave you time."

"Yeah." Dalton looked at her legs. "I . . . I don't think now's a good time."

Giana's face dropped. Her eyes narrowed.

Dalton figured she wanted him to explain himself. "It's just . . . work and stuff."

"Dalton, work is not going anywhere."

He wondered if she could see where he was going with this.

"Fine." Giana stood as the Shuttle came to the next stop. She walked back to her seat closer to the front of the Shuttle.

Dalton watched her smile as she sat back down next to her friends.

As far as he was concerned, they had broken up for a second time even though they had never really gotten back together. He felt an ache in his chest and something stale in his mouth.

When the Shuttle stopped at Sector 14, Giana and her friends got off. Dalton hesitated, but then he remembered he told Ayden he would meet him here.

* * *

Ayden bit into his sandwich. The contents of the sandwich were falling out onto the plate.

Dalton had finished his meal at lightning speed. It was nearing 2 P.M. "I saw someone in the Safe Way last night. I think he was following me."

Ayden swallowed the bite he'd been chewing. "What?"

"In the Safe Way last night, I saw—"

"Wait! You were in the Safe Way last night?"

"Yeah."

"In Sector 6?"

"That's where I live so . . . yeah."

"There was an air leak in the Safe Way in Sector 6 last night. It was all over the news. They were shuttling people to the Community House. People got sick, some died. I heard they just fixed it late this morning."

"I didn't get sick."

Ayden shook his head. "Man . . ."

Dalton was staring past Ayden at the display of greens, growing under bright, fluorescent lights. People were taking the greens and putting them in their salad bowls and on their sandwiches.

"I mean . . ." Ayden chewed another bite from his sandwich. "They must have put out signs and stuff too."

"It was dark," said Dalton.

"I'm sure they put it up on the Mega Screen."

"Mega Screen malfunctioned."

Ayden leaned forward. "The Mega Screen malfunctioned?"

"Yeah."

Ayden leaned back. "I *told* Derek we need a new one every year."

Ayden's eyes followed Dalton's, and he turned around. Giana and her friends had headed for the salad bar.

"It's still bothering you, huh?"

"You know that song by the Embers," said Dalton. "Remember the one that was playing when we went to that bar in Sector 16?"

"No."

"It was the one about the big light in the air and the clouds . . . white ones."

"Okay." Ayden balled up the paper his sandwich had been wrapped in.

"I dreamed about it last night . . . the Sun, and I was running through a field of plants that grew from the ground. There was running water . . . I mean through the green—"

"It's just a song, man."

"I know, but do you ever have dreams like that? Like that kinda shit?"

Ayden shook his head. "Sometimes I have dreams of being on the Mega Screen."

Dalton swept his gloved knuckle across his lips. "I think there's more to it. I can feel it."

"You okay, man? How much blood did you lose?"

* * *

Dalton was relieved Giana wasn't on the Shuttle. At first, he wondered if she was trying to avoid him by taking another car or getting on at a different time, but then he realized it was Thursday. Classes at the Secondary School ran Monday, Wednesday, Friday or Tuesday, Thursday, Saturday. Giana chose the former schedule.

She had probably invited her friends to the apartment her parents paid for in Sector 3. She said it was hers until she took her competencies. If Dalton could have an apartment like that, he would never take his competencies.

As they were cleaning the filters on Tower 5, Dalton asked, "Hey, did you ever find that guy, Glenn?"

"Nah," said Ran-Ran. "Don't know what happened to him. Figured he might be dead under all that rubble, but when they cleared it this morning, they didn't find no body."

"Maybe he . . . left?"

"The way you said you saw him, crouching in that rubble like that, gave me the chills. I had nightmares last night."

Dalton shook his head. "I don't know what he was doing."

"The work was too hard." Felix took the clean filter from Dalton and handed him another to clean. "That little guy knew he couldn't last another day doing what we do."

"I don't think that's driving people away," said Ran-Ran. "It's the lack of recognition. I mean, we keep this place running. Without us, this stuff would be in people's homes." He waved his hand through the dirt cloud, making the debris twist and twirl.

"How's your hand doing, boy?"

"It's fine. Still hurts." Dalton was using his left hand as a crutch. He couldn't even grip things in his right. When he got to the changing room, he wrapped a fresh roll of gauze around it. The blood was bright red and pus came out of the cut when he pressed on his palm. He smothered it in disinfectant, using the whole bottle.

* * *

Dalton yawned as he exited the Shuttle. Entering the Safe Way, he checked for any warning signs and glanced up at the Mega Screen.

The hallway was empty, but the Mega Screen was blaring a late-night comedy show. It was a re-run of old jokes Dalton had fallen asleep to a dozen times.

"Hey!" A woman was leaning against the window. He hadn't noticed her. He was glad to see she wasn't wearing a gas mask. She was thin and wore a ribbed tank top. Her oversized pants were held up by thick suspenders. Her hair was short, shaved on the sides and the back with a tuft of longer hair on top of her head.

She held something in her hand. She pressed down on it, and the Mega Screen was silenced.

"How did you . . ."

She put her finger to his lips. "They listen in here." She pressed the button again, and the Mega Screen blared back to life. "That was just to get your attention." Her voice was a whisper.

"What do you want from me?"

"Five minutes."

She was standing incredibly close, but Dalton didn't smell any fruity scents or sweet-smelling shampoos. Instead, he felt heat radiating off her like he was standing next to a furnace.

Do I really want this strange woman in my apartment? She had a sense of urgency in her eyes that gave him chills. He thought about grabbing her around the waist and lifting her onto his countertop.

Dalton shook his head. Surely that's not what she came for. He was curious.

He walked with her to his apartment. He put his access card in the door slot. *Maybe I should warn her about the cockroaches*, he thought. He had never had a woman in his apartment. He walked in and stood against the wall. He held his hand against the door slot to stop it from sliding shut.

She didn't seem to notice.

She had a tattoo of a green bird etched into the back of her head, visible through her stubble-short hair.

Dalton closed the door.

She was looking around the apartment under the couch, under the cushions on the couch. She rummaged through the cabinets.

"Can you tell me what you're doing?"

"What model is this?" She pointed to his television.

He eyed her.

She picked up the display box. "Better safe than sorry I guess." She smashed the television box down on the table that served as an entertainment center.

"Hey, what the hell?" Before Dalton could say anything else, she had quickly and efficiently dismantled the box and crushed what was left under her heavy boot.

"What did you do that for?" Dalton's hand was still on his forehead. He stared at where his television box had been obliterated.

"The newer models are bugged." She put the palms of her hands against the counter and lifted herself on top of it. She sat with her feet dangling high off the floor.

"Believe me that wasn't a new model."

"Let's get to the point. My name's Myha Morgan, and I didn't just come here to break your television."

Dalton shook his head.

"You should sit," she said.

"I'll stand by the door, thanks."

"They've been lying to us."

"Lying to us? About what?"

"About all this." She waved her hand around.

"All this?" Dalton raised his eyebrow.

"Stop repeating what I'm saying, and listen to me. They're lying by omission. They want to keep us in this place. In this *one* city . . ."

"Wait, look, I'm sorry for interrupting, but I don't understand. They? You mean the Assembly? What do you mean this *one* city? UTC Z3T is the *only* city."

She looked off to the side. "No, it isn't the *only* city, and I'm not talking about the Assembly. I'm talking about the four men who really run this place."

A roach scurried across the table, and Myha smashed it with her fist. She wiped her hand with the dish rag.

Dalton stared at where the smashed remains of the roach colored his countertop.

"Okay. Why are you telling *me* this?" he asked.

"Because you saw it, the light in the tunnel."

"Yeah, I saw a light in a tunnel. Who cares?"

Myha got down from the counter and in a few strides, her chest was a hair's breath away from his. She was looking up at him so close he could feel her breath on his face. "I do."

She stepped back and pressed something in the palm of her hand. A holograph image appeared above her palm. It was a map. It showed a system of tunnels underneath the city. Tunnels no one knew about.

"Where did you get that?"

She turned and walked away from him. "There's a lot more I could tell you." She had her back to him. "But you'll have to come with me."

The girl had just smashed his television to pieces and crushed a cockroach with her bare hands. But something about this girl intrigued him. Plus, if he went with her, she might not break anything else in his apartment.

"Fine," said Dalton.

"Hope you cleaned the filters on your air mask."

*   *   *

They took the Air Shuttle to Sector 14. Dalton tried to ask more questions, but Myha put her finger to his lips. They sat in silence.

Myha didn't wear any makeup. She didn't have any perfume on and didn't use heavily scented shampoo either. She did have a locket around her neck. The tiny vibrations of the Shuttle made the locket shutter against her chest.

The Shuttle stopped, and the monitor read Sector 14 in bright red letters.

"Come on." Myha got up from her seat.

Sector 14 wasn't bustling like it was in the waking hours, but there were a fair number of people eating at the cafeteria tables. Most of them ate alone. *Probably have apartments infested with cockroaches*, Dalton thought.

Myha passed through the rows of round tables to the elevator. Dalton followed her. He felt oddly comfortable following this strange girl through the amber lit Sector 14 in the early morning hours. It put him in a strange mood. *Maybe I'm just delirious or maybe I* do *have an infection.* He looked down at his hand. The blood was seeping through the gauze again. He hadn't thought to put his gloves back on before they left his apartment.

Myha had on a pair of fingerless gloves.

Once they were in the elevator, instead of pressing one button, she pressed a series of buttons.

What is she doing? Dalton wondered.

Normally the buttons would stay lit until they reached that floor, but as soon as Myha pressed them, the buttons no longer glowed. She was fast, not even Dalton remembered the exact number sequence.

The elevator lurched downwards. Dalton felt air under his feet.

"You should put your air mask on now." Myha was putting on hers. She had a pair of goggles that were separate from her mask, which only covered her nose and mouth.

Dalton put on his air mask as they descended.

The elevator jerked to a stop. He felt it go down a couple more feet, gently this time, and then the solid ding, and the door of the elevator opened.

They were outside. No Safe Way greeted them.

This wasn't unfamiliar to Dalton. His job required him to be outside. Even for hoverboard racing, it was necessary to be outside. Of course, hoverboard racing was illegal.

He followed Myha and watched the dust play around her body.

They stood in front of a building.

"What Sector is this?" asked Dalton.

"It isn't one." Myha scanned her access card on the display screen on the side of the building. The airlock opened, and they stepped inside.

6

They walked into the building. Myha pulled her mask and goggles down so they dangled from her neck right above her locket. Dalton took off his mask as well.

They were in a large room with rows of seating separated by a carpeted aisle. The room was lit by bright standing fluorescents. The lights were hooked up to a humming generator.

There were stains on the walls that Dalton imagined were once white, but now had turned some yellow color that looked like the puke of someone who hadn't eaten. Graffiti covered some of the yellow.

What might have once been beautiful gold trim lining the walls was now flaking gold trim. The seats had some of the plush torn out. In the back of the room was a stage with old, faded curtains hanging from the rafters.

On the stage, a group of people talked and sat on plastic chairs that had survived the wear and torment of their plush cousins. There were roughly a dozen people up there. Dalton couldn't see them very well from where he and Myha were standing, but as they walked closer to the stage, Dalton recognized Jareth and his crew. They looked at him as he approached. Jareth's expression didn't change.

Some members of the large group stopped talking as Dalton approached and stared at him. Dalton tried not to make eye contact with any of them.

His shoes stuck to the carpet as he walked. It wasn't soft, but was thin and hard like there was cement underneath.

The room was hot, and the air felt heavy. Dalton wondered which tower filtered the air in this building. Maybe this crew had found a way to do it themselves?

Myha pulled herself up onto the stage. She reached down a hand to Dalton. He shook his head and pulled himself up.

The floor of the stage was hard, uncarpeted. Computers and monitors were set up in the back. Someone sat close to the monitors. Someone Dalton could not make out due to the number of people standing and sitting around him on the small stage.

Glenn? It was the skinny man who went missing his first day on the job. Dalton hadn't seen him with his oxygen mask off, but he recognized his wiry, short frame. His body was even smaller without the hazmat suit on.

But there was something strange about him now. He seemed to hold himself differently.

"Welcome." His voice was surprisingly deep. Dalton couldn't remember hearing him speak the first time they met.

"Hey." Dalton narrowed his eyes.

He looked around at the others, wondering if they were going to jump him. Dalton suddenly felt naked. He didn't have a knife on him or anything. Not that he was in the habit of carrying a knife, but maybe he should have grabbed a sharp one from his kitchen before he left his apartment.

He glanced over at Myha. Her expression didn't read, *"They're going to jump you."* He trusted her. He hadn't met any other girl like her.

"It took Myha a pretty minute to get you here." Glenn stood. He was a head shorter than Dalton, but no one spoke while he was speaking. "You need to sit down."

"Who are you?" Dalton asked. It can't be Glenn. Glenn was a quiet man, a timid man. Not the type of man who would boss around someone larger than him. *This* Glenn would have backhanded Felix for correcting him.

"My name is Glenn Sutton."

"Why did you bring me here?" Dalton asked.

Glenn turned to Myha. "Did you show him the map?"

"Yeah, I did."

"I think he needs to see it again." Glenn stepped back.

Myha removed the glove from her left hand and pressed down on her palm. An image of the city was projected from her hand, glowing from her skin. It was the same image she had briefly showed him back at the apartment.

He thought it was coming from some kind of disk or something, but the light emitted from under her skin. The blood vessels in her hand were visible as the light shone through the thin membrane.

"What do you think that is?" asked Glenn.

"It's a map of the city," said Dalton.

"And what about these?" Glenn pointed to the tunnels beneath the ground and the buildings.

Dalton narrowed his eyes at Glenn. "Tunnels, I guess."

"You work outside, Dalton. Have you ever heard of tunnels under the city?"

"No."

Myha's right hand was nearing her palm. Glenn grabbed her wrist. "Wait! Let it finish loading."

Words hovered over the map.

URGENT: GUIDELINES FOR EVACUATION

IF YOU ARE READING THIS, THE SENSORS LOCATED OUTSIDE UNITED TRACE Z3T HAVE DETECTED THAT THE LAND IS ONCE AGAIN HABITABLE. IT IS IMPERATIVE THAT YOU EXIT IMMEDIATELY AS UNITED TRACE Z3T WAS

DESIGNED AS A TEMPORARY SAFE HOUSE AND IS NOT SUITABLE FOR LONG-TERM HABITATION.

TWO ACCESS KEYS WILL ACTIVATE THE EXIT DOOR.

THE EXIT IS LOCATED IN THE CITY'S EXISTING SEWAGE TUNNELS. THERE ARE DESIGNATED DOORS TO THE TUNNELS LOCATED AT THE GLOWING POINTS ON THE MAP BELOW.

PROCEED THROUGH THESE DOORS AND INTO THE TUNNELS. THE EXIT IS INDICATED BY THE ORANGE SQUARE ON THE MAP.

PLACE THE ACCESS KEYS INTO THE LOCKING MECHANISM AND TURN EACH KEY TWO ROTATIONS CLOCKWISE.

EXIT IN AN ORDERLY FASHION.

CONGRATULATIONS UNITED TRACE Z3T. YOU SURVIVED AND CAN BEGIN TO REBUILD.

Not suitable for long-term habitation. Dalton read the words again. How long ago were we supposed to leave?

"How do I know this thing is real?" asked Dalton.

Myha pressed down her palm and clenched her hand. "It is." She put the glove back on.

"How long have you known about this?"

"Long enough," Glenn said.

Tunnels under the city. Locking mechanisms. "It was you," said Dalton. "You lured me to that spot. You knew I would fall in, didn't you?"

"If you wouldn't have fallen in," said Glenn, "you wouldn't know what we know now."

"Why would you want to leave United Trace?" asked Dalton. "Don't any of you call this home?"

"It's a failing city," said Myha. "Do you really want to be here when everything goes to shit?"

"I think this city has gone pass its deadline already," said Dalton. "Do your parents remember anything else? Do your grandparents?"

Myha stepped up to him and looked up into his face. "They lied to us. They teach little kids that the outside air is worse than it is in here. They teach us that humanity was supposed to live on under this concrete tomb. The only reason we have this," Myha pointed to her palm, "is because there are devices outside this prison that detected clean air, livable conditions. We were supposed to leave when this map was released, but someone wanted to keep it from us. Someone hid it."

"What does it matter?" Dalton shook his head. "Even if I believe you, there's no way we're getting out. We need two access keys. I don't see any of those lying around."

Glenn reached inside his shirt and pulled out a chain. At the end of the chain was a silver key.

"So, you have one." Dalton folded his arms.

"We've looked for the other one," said Myha. "But we haven't had any luck."

"So, there you go." Dalton turned away from them.

"You're right," said Myha. "We'll probably never find the key, but there is something else we can do."

"What's that?"

"We can blow up the MCG."

"The main city generator?"

"Yes," she said. "If we could turn off the city's power, there goes their giant Band-Aid. Without that generator, there won't be enough power to circulate the air, to grow the food, to transport people between sectors."

Glenn put the key back under his shirt. "It's the best chance we got to get out of here. We're going to have to force them out. Then, whoever has the other key will have to reveal it or he'll die with everyone else. That's why we have to break into Eskov and blow up the MCG."

"And this guy is friends with the Director's brother." Jareth's voice hit Dalton's ears.

Why would I want to be part of an operation that this guy's a part of? "You people are crazy." Dalton turned around to face them. "You put together this whole frickin' elaborate nonsense. Good work, Jareth, by the way. You had me going for about a second."

Dalton jumped down from the stage.

"This isn't a joke, Dalton Anderson," Myha's voice rang out.

"Well, it sure is *funny*." Dalton put on his air mask and pressed the button on the side of the airlock. The door hissed open.

7

Dalton opened the door to his apartment and slipped his access card back into his pocket.

The roach Myha had smashed with her fist was still dead on the countertop. His television was in pieces on the floor next to one of the couch cushions.

He grabbed a bowl and a spoon and set them down on the counter. He opened the cabinet and remembered he had thrown out his last box of cereal.

Dalton sighed.

He smelled copper. Blood was dripping from his bandaged hand. It stained the side of his pants. Dalton grabbed a fistful of cloth napkins and pressed them into his hand. He cringed from the pain, but hoped the blood would stop.

His stomach rumbled. He looked in the fridge. It was bare, except for one carton of orange juice. Dalton drank what was left in the carton, which wasn't much.

He walked over to the couch and tossed the discarded cushion back where it belonged. He laid down and closed his eyes.

* * *

The doorbell buzzed. At first, Dalton could hear it in his dream. Then, in that place between sleep and wake he could hear it in the hazy corners of his mind.

Dalton blinked.

The buzzing came again, and Dalton opened his eyes. He looked at his access card. He had a few missed calls from Ayden.

It was probably him at the door. He was most likely wondering why Dalton hadn't called to hang out on his day off.

The buzzing continued as Dalton got up to answer the door.

He pulled open the door and standing there was . . . Jareth.

Dalton started to pull the door closed.

Jareth stopped it with his hand. "Look, I just wanna talk."

"Well, I'm done," said Dalton. "Ha-ha. You got me."

"I know you're not stupid, okay? I'm here because it took a lot of convincing to get me to believe it too."

"How do you know where I live?" In two years, I hadn't told Giana that one.

"What? You think we haven't been watching you? Look, we thought about your friend, Ayden, is it? His brother's access card can open any door in Eskov. But they'd never side with us.

Derek Haley's Director now. He's not going to compromise that because we tell him to. You could convince Ayden to let us use the card."

"Why would I do that?"

"Because you know what's at stake. You pretend like you don't care what's going on in this city. Well, I think that's bullshit and so does Glenn."

"You're crazy."

"Maybe. But I didn't volunteer to come here just to go back to my crew empty handed."

"What do you want?"

"Your stomach is growling louder than the volume on the Mega Screen. Let's grab some food."

* * *

Dalton grabbed three fries from his plate, dipped them in copious amounts of ketchup, and finished them off in three bites. He wiped his mouth with the back of his hand.

"You know," said Jareth, "you look around a lot when you eat."

They sat at one of the tables in the corner of the cafeteria in Sector 14.

Jareth leaned back in his chair. "Now, that you got some food in you. I guess your brain will be working a little better."

Dalton didn't look at him. He continued to scoff down his food.

"Myha didn't tell you how she got that map under her skin?"

Dalton kept eating. Jareth didn't wait for an answer.

"Her parents were Drs. Holland and Rebecca Morgan. Supposedly, they found out about the map's existence and went to the Assembly. They were even guests on a talk show, telling everyone about the world outside the city and that it was safe to go there. How ridiculous it all was that the people who built this place to protect us from a catastrophic event would intend for us to remain here forever. But her parents were slandered. Members of the Assembly tried to discredit them. Then, they just . . . disappeared."

Dalton swallowed. "They never showed anyone the map?"

"I don't know," said Jareth. "They had to hide it so it wouldn't be destroyed. They put it in Myha's hand and stitched it up. It had healed by the time they went missing, and Myha always wears gloves to hide it. They gave her the key too. She lets Glenn wear it because she doesn't feel safe holding two parts of the secret."

"Why don't you just tell everybody?"

Jareth shook his head. "Two educated doctors couldn't convince them that it was real."

"But they didn't show the people the map or the instructions. So what if the Assembly saw it."

"We can't show anybody the map." Jareth leaned forward. "Not yet. First, we must convince them that leaving the city is something they *have* to do. Right now, they look at all these frickin' distractions. No one thinks they're going to die. No one sees how bad things really are. This has been their whole life. Buying things, watching the Mega Screen, updating their air filters. You think we can just show them some map, and they'll all suddenly be on board?"

"Maybe you're not giving them enough credit. Myha and Glenn were able to convince *you*."

Jareth smirked. "Alright, Test-Tube, you wanna help me with something. I'm going to need an extra pair of hands, and yours look like they could do the job. Well, maybe not the one in that bloodied bandage. I can see why you're trying to hide it."

Dalton furrowed his brow. *If this is some elaborate joke, I should let him have it. He's trying way too hard.*

"It's not a joke." Myha's words echoed in his head. She sounded so sincere.

It doesn't make sense. Why would they want to keep us here? Then again it doesn't make sense that this was supposed to be permanent either. Every year, the air was getting more leaden with debris. People were dying from breathing in *air*.

Dalton remembered his dream. He was breathing freely without an air mask. Everything was open. No concrete dome loomed above him.

Why do I put on an air mask? To provide a temporary solution when I walk outside because the air is dangerous to me. But when I'm inside, I take the mask off because the air is no longer dangerous to me. They were supposed to leave. It made sense. They couldn't be the last trace of humanity in a doomed city. They were meant to rebuild.

"Dalton, are you coming?"

Dalton looked across the cafeteria. Giana and her friends stood at the salad bar. They had spotted Dalton and Jareth. They were pointing at them and talking.

Dalton got up from his seat. "Sure. Let's just get out of here."

* * *

Dalton breathed in through his air mask. He and Jareth had arrived at a large warehouse on the outskirts of the city. It towered above the city walls with their massive piles of debris.

Many older buildings in the city had been abandoned for one reason or another. Dalton imagined Glenn's theater and this warehouse were two such buildings. But it looked like they had managed to clear out the bad air, perhaps through some homemade filtration system.

Dalton and Jareth entered a rusty air lock. Dalton wondered how efficient it really was. He hoped it was more effective than he thought.

The warehouse had stacks upon stacks of discarded parts, metals, and plastics. Shelves and large buckets were stocked with items.

"You're looking around like you've never been here before." Jareth walked alongside Dalton as he gazed around the room.

"I haven't."

"Where do you get your hoverboard parts?"

"I find them myself. I've spent hours sifting through the junk in those dirt piles outside the walls."

"Geez, no wonder your hoverboard looks like crap."

"I wouldn't be able to afford this anyway. I'm having enough trouble paying the rent on my apartment."

"I don't think that's your apartment, man. I think that apartment belongs to a family of cockroaches. A mama and papa, and their hundred or so kids. I saw like five of those bastards in the corner by your dirty laundry, and I didn't get past the door."

Jareth was tall, taller even than Dalton. "Hey, why do *you* follow a man like Glenn? Why does everyone respect him so much?"

"Glenn? He infiltrated every major position in the city. He knows more about UTC than you wanna know. He spent two weeks out in the dirt piles with no food or water, searching for the way out of this place. If that doesn't deserve some sort of respect, I don't know what does."

Beyond the rows of shelves was a large counter. A young boy, maybe twelve or thirteen, stood behind it. His head was bald, and he wore an orange jumpsuit.

Jareth leaned his elbow on the counter. "Hey, Chad. Slow day?"

"Yep." Chad was mixing two substances together in a beaker.

"What is that?" Dalton asked.

Chad looked up. "Who's this guy?"

"He's a friend of mine."

"He checks out?"

"He checks out."

"It's glycerin and nitric acid. It makes nitroglycerin," Chad said.

"What's nitroglycerin?" asked Dalton.

"A highly explosive substance." Chad didn't take his eyes off what he was doing. "You let some cotton balls soak this stuff up, mix it with some sodium nitrate, and you got yourself a party."

Dalton stepped back from the table.

Jareth didn't seem fazed. "Look, Chad, I'm in the market for some powerful explosives."

"What do you need?"

"I'm talking enough to blow up one floor of an apartment complex."

Chad looked up at him. "You're talking about more than a hundred pounds of dynamite. What do you need it for?"

Jareth put his access card on the table. "Take whatever you think is fair."

The door behind the counter opened. A large man ambled out. "What's up, Loco?" The big man patted Chad on the shoulder.

"Come on, Grim. Don't call me Loco. It's Chad or Flash."

"Alright, Loco." Grim extended his hand to Jareth. Jareth shook his hand. "Jareth, my man. Anything this man wants, Loco, you give it to him. He's one of us."

"He wants dynamite," said Chad.

"Well, give it to him." The large man swung his head around to Chad.

"He wants over a hundred pounds of dynamite."

"What you need that much dynamite for, my friend?" asked Grim.

"Look," Jareth slid his access card across the table, "whatever it's worth to you, I'll pay extra if you leave that up to me."

They were silent for a moment.

"Okay." Grim nodded his head. "Loco, load 'em up."

Chad loaded their bags with the dynamite. His small hands worked slowly and precisely.

Jareth picked his card up from the table and handed it to Chad.

Chad tossed it back to him. "I already charged your card."

"How much did you charge me?"

"You leave that up to me."

Dalton shouldered his bag. It was heavy, but manageable. Dalton was wondering how Jareth could just throw money at people like that. Maybe it wasn't all his. The rest of the crew might have chipped in for this.

* * *

Dalton and Jareth put down the backpacks on the stage. The others weren't there, but Myha and Glenn were. Myha sat in a plastic chair with her elbows on her knees. Glenn was sitting by the computer.

Dalton hadn't noticed it before, but there was a piano on the stage. It was partly hidden by the curtains.

"I see you changed your mind," said Myha, looking down at Dalton from the stage. "Jareth told us he would convince you."

"I don't know if I'm cool with this," said Dalton. "You're talking about some pretty out-there stuff and you're dealing with it in a very dangerous way."

Glenn stepped to the edge of the stage. "I know you're tired of wiping down those filters only to see them suck up the cloud of debris you just wiped away."

"Your friend," said Myha, "you have to convince him to help us. Blowing up the MCG is the only way."

8

Dalton held his hand above his head. He hoped it would stop the bleeding. The Shuttle was packed. A baby's cries were coming from the front of the Shuttle. His cries were muffled by the air mask, which he was trying to pull off his face with his fat, little hands.

His mother pulled his hands away from the mask. Adults and older children didn't need to wear air masks in the Shuttle and Safe Ways, but infants were more susceptible to minute amounts of pollution that got in from time to time.

Dalton pulled his access card out of his phone and scrolled for Ayden's name. A hologram image of Ayden's face appeared above his access card, and Dalton pressed "call."

"Hey, man. What took you so long to call back?"

"I've been busy." Blood trickled down Dalton's arm.

"I called and texted you like half a dozen times over the last two days. Is your card malfunctioning or something?"

"No, I've just been busy."

"Yeah, you said that. Okay, man, no big. I just wanted to see if you wanted to hang out, but if you're too busy, I'll chill here on the Xeclade."

"Can we meet at my apartment?"

"*Your* apartment?"

Dalton laughed. "Yeah, the cockroach motel. No, ah . . . I wanted to grab something to eat anyway, so I was thinking we could meet at my place and then go to Sector 14, grab a bite to eat. I heard about that new comedy show, a lot of crude humor, right up your alley."

"You know it. Okay. Sounds good. I'll meet you there in maybe thirty minutes. I gotta finish this game. Later."

Dalton put his access card back in his pocket as the Shuttle slowed to a stop outside Sector 6. He walked to his apartment.

He figured since they would be staying there a little while, he'd clean the roach guts off the counter and sweep up what was left of his television. He didn't want Ayden asking questions about that. He didn't have much time. Chad warned them that dynamite doesn't keep well. Myha was always at the theater. If that dynamite exploded, it would be like a giant fist coming down and splattering *her* to pieces.

What am I going to say? Dalton wondered. Hey, man, I need your brother's access card. My new friends and I wanna blow up the MCG. Geez . . . he's going to think I'm crazy.

He and Ayden had been friends for over a decade. If Ayden told him all this, Dalton liked to think he would believe him.

His doorbell buzzed.

Dalton opened the door.

"Hey, man." Ayden gave Dalton a high-five that ended in a firm hand squeeze. He plopped down on the couch.

Dalton sat on one of the bar stools by the counter.

"I got a new Xeclade." Ayden turned his head to Dalton. He had his arms spread from one end of the couch to the other.

"Again?"

"Yeah, thing's a piece of junk. They keep breaking, you know. It's like they were designed to break so I would have to buy a new one."

Dalton grinned and rubbed the side of his head. "Dude."

"Hey, what happened to your T.V.?"

Dalton shook his head, his mouth thin-lipped. "Broke," he said.

"Technology." Ayden turned around on the couch. "Well, you got nothing to watch. You ready to get out of here."

"Ah . . . yeah, I just wanted to talk to you about something first."

"Sure, man. What's going on?"

Dalton sighed, nodded his head, and looked down at the floor. "This is going to sound crazy. I, uh, met these *people*. Well . . . this girl."

"Oh, really? What's she like?"

"No, it wasn't like that."

"Okay . . ."

"She's got this map. It shows tunnels under the city. Like the one I fell in. And there are instructions above the map, instructions for evacuating the city."

Ayden raised an eyebrow.

"I know how it sounds, but this map . . . it was only released once these detectors determined that the environment outside the city was livable."

"What are you talking about, man?"

"I'm talking about leaving the city. I've cleaned those air filters for two years, and in two years the air has gotten ten times worse. It only makes sense that the city wasn't designed to be permanent. That's why the map and the instructions were made so we could go outside again once everything was over."

"But, Dalt, you don't know *who* made that map you saw. What if this girl you met made it herself? What if it's some big joke?"

"I thought so at first. I kinda didn't want to believe it. But it's real. How would they have known about the tunnels? Why does it all make so much sense?"

"Maybe . . . you're forcing it to make sense. I mean, so what if the air's bad? That doesn't mean that it's safe out there. We're supposed to be here. We're the last trace of humanity and all that crap. We're here because whatever the world used to be is gone, man. And some map ain't gonna change that."

"But how do you *know*?"

Ayden shrugged. "I've lived here my whole life. This is it. Look, I understand, there must be a lot of people who think that there might be something better out there, but they let that thought pass, and they get on with their lives. Man, you got a shit apartment and a shit job. I guess I get why you've caught onto this idea."

"This isn't because I hate my life, Ayden. If you were in a burning building, would you just shrug your shoulders and say 'well that's life'? You would get outta there."

"We're not in a burning building, Dalt. I'm not dying. I've got my life and my stupid brother and my Xeclade and the Mega Screen. I've got the clothes on my back. I'm breathing healthy. We got food here and water. We got everything we need right here. Out there? We don't know what's out there. What if you go out there, and you can't come back? And what if it's worse than it is here?"

"Eventually, it's going to fall apart," said Dalton. "The air filters are overtaxed. Soon, it's going to take more and more energy to power them. We can't recycle the air forever. People are dying from it. The building *is* on fire."

Ayden put his hand up in the air and brought it back down. "Okay, so what are you going to do about it?"

"We want to shut down the MCG."

Ayden's eyes grew wide.

"The crew thinks it's the only way to convince everyone to leave," said Dalton. "If we shut down the MCG, the other generators won't be strong enough to power the whole city. The lights will go out, they won't be able to grow food or power the water filtration plant or keep the bad air out of the Safe Ways."

"You're kidding me, right?"

Dalton shook his head. "We need to leave, and the only way we're getting to the MCG is if we have access to Eskov."

Ayden stood. "You're telling me this because you want me to steal Derek's access card."

"I'd be telling you anyway. I want you to get out too."

"No way, man. Look, I think you need sleep and food. I think you should go to a doctor about that hand."

Dalton looked down at his hand. Blood was dripping onto the countertop where it rested.

"I'm going to let you do that." Ayden walked to the door. "See ya later, man." He shut it behind him.

Dalton shook his head and rubbed his knuckle across his lips.

Jareth had given him the code for the elevator. Dalton entered it and walked to the crew's headquarters.

Myha was on the stage. Next to her a man sat at the computer. Dalton pulled himself up onto the stage.

"Dalton?" Myha's eyes were glued to the screen. She had her hand on the man's shoulder as she leaned forward.

"Yeah," said Dalton.

"This is Shrink." She motioned her head to the man at the computer. Shrink was slightly overweight. He wore his shirt tucked in, which only made his stomach look more pronounced.

"Hey." He didn't tear his eyes away from his work as he rapidly hit the keys on the keyboard. He had on glasses with darkened lenses. His fingers paused on the keyboard to take a puff from his vapor stick. Then he was hammering away at the keys again.

"He's our resident hacker. Remember when I controlled the Mega Screen? That was all him. Right now, he's working on something that will allow us to scramble the cameras in Eskov."

"About that," said Dalton.

"What?" Myha stepped away from the computer and faced Dalton. Her eyes were piercing.

"I talked to Ayden."

"What did he say? Is he going to get us the access card?"

Dalton shook his head. "I don't think so."

"You have to talk to him again."

"I know Ayden," said Dalton. "He's not going to come around if I pester him."

Myha looked at him. Her mouth formed a hard line.

"Where's Glenn?" Dalton asked.

Myha turned back to the computer. "He's visiting his mom."

"Okay." Dalton looked across the room at the bags of dynamite resting against the wall. "Are you sure you want to be here?"

"It's not like we can do this in one of *their* buildings," said Myha. "Talking about our plans is one thing, but putting them into action in a place that could be bugged is another."

"What Sector do you live in?"

"I live here," said Myha. "So does Glenn."

So, that's it, Dalton thought. She is with Glenn.

"Okay, um, I gotta go," said Dalton. "The roaches are getting really bad in my apartment.

Dalton jumped off the stage and headed for the door. He shook his head. *Why did I mention the roaches?*

* * *

Dalton grabbed a bottle of roach spray and some traps. He brought the items up to the man at the counter.

The man had a grizzled beard. There was a half-eaten sandwich on the counter. He started ringing up the bottle of spray and the traps.

"Forty-two," he said.

Dalton was eyeing the selection of pocket knives behind the glass.

The man followed his gaze. "Interested?"

"Sure."

The man swiped his access card and unlocked the case from behind the counter. He picked up one of the knives and ran his finger along the dull edge of the blade. "This one's the

Armageddon Alpha 4. It has a three-inch blade. Closed length is five inches. Made of the sharpest stainless steel. Here give it a feel." He handed the pocket knife to Dalton.

Dalton was surprised by how light it felt. It fit perfectly in his pocket. He handed the knife back to the man. "Ring this up for me."

"Sure thing."

Dalton handed the man his access card. Before ringing him up, the man paused and looked at his card then back at Dalton. His face held a look of discernment peppered with distain.

Dalton knew instinctively that the man had glanced at the three extra numbers separated from the long string of numbers in his identification code. These numbers marked him as an artificial birth. Maybe that really was one of the shop owner's best knives, and he just sold it to a Test-Tube Baby.

Dalton took the Shuttle back to his apartment. He threw his bag on the couch. He had the knife in his pocket.

He didn't see any roaches in the corner. It was as if they knew he had come to annihilate them. *That's why they live so long*, he thought. *They run. They fit into small spaces and hide.*

He heard ringing. He picked up his access card. He didn't look at the caller.

"Hello?"

"Hi, man." Ayden's voice came over the line.

"Hey. What's up?" Dalton tried to sound natural, like Ayden hadn't looked at him like he was crazy hours earlier and left him to *chill*.

"Man, I was thinking about what you said. I mean, it's crazy, but I don't know. I guess I was just weirded out by the whole thing. I still kinda am. But you're like the smartest guy I know. I don't wanna be looking back in ten years, choking on the crap in the air, wishing I would've believed you. Look, I'll get you the card. But, you have to promise me something."

"What's that?"

"Promise me it's not the blood loss."

Dalton laughed. "No, it's not the blood loss."

"Okay then. I'm in."

9

Dalton went back to the crew's hangout. He figured Myha would be there, and he needed to get the details for the job so he could pass the information along to Ayden. He wanted to make sure they moved that dynamite as soon as possible.

As he exited the airlock, he was greeted by music. It was gentle and graceful, like a whisper. He had never heard music like that before.

On the stage, Glenn sat at the old piano; his fingers danced on the keys, slowly, methodically. In that moment, Dalton felt like he knew him better than anybody.

Myha sat in the darkness in the row of seats furthest away from the stage. She listened in silence. Even after Dalton sat next to her, she didn't speak for some time. Her eyes were glassy.

"He plays when it's too much," she said. "When he's stressed."

"He's good," said Dalton.

She nodded. "He used to play for the Caustic Embers before they hit the Mega Screen. Once the Assembly started telling them what to do with their music, he left. It just makes me so angry," she said. "They tell us whether it's night or day with their fluorescents. The Sun could be out right now, and we wouldn't know."

"Ayden agreed to do it."

"You should tell him."

Glenn had his head down. He hadn't looked at them. He probably hadn't noticed them sitting there in the dark, watching him play.

"Okay." Dalton got up from his seat and approached the stage. He pulled himself up and walked to the piano.

Glenn still had not looked up.

"He wants in," said Dalton.

Glenn continued to play. "That's good. We'll meet at Eskov tomorrow night."

"Okay."

Dalton stood with his hands in his pockets. He felt kind of awkward standing next to Glenn while he played.

"You know," said Glenn. "I lost my mom. She went insane, wanting to get out of this place." His eyes were distant. "She ran outside . . . without an air mask." A tear rolled down his cheek, and he gulped. "I couldn't find her. They said she choked on the debris. They revived her, put her on life support. She's been that way for ten years. When we blow this thing. The machines that are keeping her alive will go out. I don't want her to die alone. Will you come with me? If I go alone, I might get selfish."

"Sure," he said. Dalton didn't have a mom. He certainly didn't know what it was like to lose one, but he could read the grief in Glenn's eyes. He was resigned to let her go.

Glenn's fingers lighted on the last notes. He shut the fallboard, sheltering the keys.

* * *

Dalton sat next to Glenn on the Air Shuttle as they traveled to Sector 9, the hospital sector. *Why didn't he ask Myha to come with him?* Dalton wondered. Maybe they weren't as close as he assumed.

They entered the cold, white hospital. The humming of breathing machines hit their ears. They went to the counter, and Glenn gave the nurse his access card.

"Your mother is in Room 8, Mr. Sutton," the nurse didn't look at him, but continued to stare at her computer monitor.

"I know," said Glenn. "I would like to talk to a doctor before seeing her."

"Okay, have a seat."

Glenn ambled over to the waiting room, and Dalton followed. They waited in silence for several, long minutes. Dalton didn't know what to say. Glenn had come here to watch his mom die. A chill ran up his spine. Dalton suddenly felt he shouldn't be here.

The doctor spoke to Glenn in his office while Dalton waited outside. He could only barely hear their voices. He couldn't make out the words.

The doctor and Glenn walked outside. The doctor put his hand on Glenn's shoulder. "I'll give you some time with her," he said. He walked back into his office.

Dalton followed Glenn to Room 8. He had his hands in his pockets. As he entered the room, a thin woman rested on a white bed. A machine beeped next to the bed. It registered her heartbeats in a series of jumping lines, like a light, little girl skipping down a narrow hallway.

Dalton found a chair in the corner of the room as Glenn sat next to his mom and took her hand.

Glenn looked up at her face. She looked like she was sleeping. Her chest rose and fell. Even in the harsh light, her cheeks were rosy. Her skin wasn't the dull gray color Dalton associated with sick, old people. It didn't look like anything was wrong with her.

Dalton found himself wondering what she was dreaming about. Was she seeing the fields of green as he had? Did old people imagine themselves young again when they dreamed? Maybe she was a little girl, leaping through the green fields, breathing fresh air.

Glenn's hand looked tense around hers. His face was peaceful, but tears ran down it. He had kept her alive here for ten years, and now he was letting her go.

The doctor came in with a nurse. They approached the bed.

"Wait," said Glenn. He got up and smoothed his mother's hair. He kissed her forehead. "Goodbye, mom." His tear fell upon her cheek and ran down her jaw.

Glenn held her hand as the nurse turned off the machine that was forcing oxygen into his mother's lungs.

A loud, long beep registered, and a flat line buzzed across the monitor. The little girl was no longer trapped in that hallway. She was free.

* * *

Dalton and Glenn sat in silence for a long time. The Shuttle stopped at four Sectors before Glenn said anything.

"Thank you."

"Yeah." Dalton put his access card away. "Why did you ask *me* to come?"

Glenn rested his head back against the seat. "It's simple really. I knew you wouldn't stop me. Maybe you would even encourage me a little if I tried to stop myself."

Dalton scratched his head. "That's sounds kind of bad that I would *encourage* you to pull the plug on your mom. I don't think I would've done that."

"It wouldn't have been bad," Glenn said. "If you think we only chose you because of your connection with Derek Haley's brother, you'd be wrong.

"I first saw you at the Community House. You fought so hard to get out of there, studying for your competencies day and night. You're smart, but you're also determined. You see a problem, and you fix it, immediately. It only took you twenty-four hours to realize this place was going down, and you didn't want to be here when it did. We've known about all this for years. We reached out to you because after sitting on our hands for all that time, we were finally ready to do something about it."

How old was Glenn? How long had Glenn been watching him?

"I don't think that's true," said Dalton. "Jareth told me that you spent weeks outside the walls of the city searching for a way out. You don't seem like the kind of guy who would wait around for someone else to save him."

Glenn turned to him and looked him straight in the eye. "You're not going to save me, Dalton. You're going to help me save myself."

* * *

The exterior of the Eskov building sank down to the ground where the debris covered its base. It towered up to the top of the concrete dome.

Dalton and Jareth carried the bags of dynamite on their backs. Shrink didn't come with them, but Myha had his scrambling device. It looked like a small remote control.

They waited in the Safe Way outside the Eskov building. Lights from under the Safe Way glowed in all directions.

Glenn wasn't looking at the Eskov building. His eyes were distant. Dalton wondered if he was still thinking about his mom. Dalton knew he must really believe in Myha's map. He kept his mom on life support for ten years and just now decided it was time. Dalton wasn't sure if he could have made that decision. Of course, blowing up the MCG would have meant making that decision anyway, only she wouldn't have died holding her son's hand.

"Is your friend coming?" asked Jareth.

"He said he would," said Dalton.

"It's been an hour and forty-five minutes. You sure he didn't get cold feet?"

Except for Shrink, Glenn's whole crew was there. Dalton didn't get a chance to meet them all in person, but he recognized their faces now. He'd never said one or two words to half a dozen of them, but, in a strange way, they were starting to feel like family. Probably because they all knew something everyone else didn't.

"He'll be here," said Dalton.

Glenn continued to gaze out the window. He didn't even look up when the conversation turned to Ayden's cold feet.

Myha wore a black jacket over her white tank top. Her back leaned against the windows of the Safe Way.

Dalton thought back on the possibility that she and Glenn were an item. They weren't affectionate towards each other. Besides living together there was no other indication they were a couple.

She was taller than Glenn. Not that that mattered. Everyone towered over Glenn, but somehow, they just didn't seem *right* together.

"Look, there he is," said Jareth.

Ayden was approaching them.

"You got the card?" Jareth asked.

"Why is *he* here?" Ayden had his hands in his pockets.

"He's part of the crew," said Dalton.

"*He's* part of the crew." Ayden raised an eyebrow.

The eyes of the whole crew were on Ayden. Dalton remembered how that had made him feel.

"Hey, do you have the access card or what?" Jareth put out his hand.

Ayden looked down at Jareth's hand and paused. He looked at the Eskov building.

Dalton followed his eyes. His heart was a lump in his throat as he watched Ayden. *He's thinking about getting out.*

"I don't know about this anymore." Ayden took a step back.

"What do you mean?" asked Dalton.

"We don't have time for this," said Jareth. "Somebody's gonna see us."

Dalton flashed his palm to Jareth.

"Why do you need to blow up the MCG?" asked Ayden.

"You know why," said Dalton.

"Why do you think *you* know what's out there?"

Dalton looked at Myha. Her eyes were wide, but she didn't say anything.

"You know what I think?" asked Ayden. "I think there's nothing out there. I think this is all just some big joke, and he's in on it." Ayden pointed to Jareth.

"It's not a joke," said Dalton.

"Man, open your eyes. He fooled around with your ex. Then, she wanted *you* back. What do you think this is?"

"It's *not* about him," said Dalton.

Ayden shook his head. "Prove me wrong. You don't have to turn off the whole city to do it. Go out there. Take some pictures or some shit. Then, come back and show me. Put it on the Mega Screen. Show everybody. Let them decide for themselves."

"They won't believe us," said Dalton. "Not unless they think it's the only way."

"Ha." Ayden took a few more steps back. He reached into his pocket and pulled out an access card. He threw it at Dalton's feet. "Whatever, man." He shrugged. "I hope you're right because if you're not," he smacked his hands together, "we're all done." He turned around and walked away.

"Wait!" Dalton yelled, but Ayden kept walking. Dalton picked up the access card. Derek's picture was in the corner.

Dalton tried to see things from Ayden's perspective. If they were wrong, Derek would lose his job. Worse, the city would go dark, and they would run out of food, water, and fresh air.

But they couldn't be wrong. They had to take the entire city with them. It wouldn't be right not to, but if they didn't see for themselves, they would never believe. The Assembly would cover it up and make them all disappear like they did to Myha's parents.

Dalton had suddenly felt an immense responsibility. He couldn't let that happen. He had never felt this much pride in anything before.

He glanced over at Myha. Her parents hid that map inside her palm for a reason. They knew they had to tell the world. They had cut into their young daughter's hand to protect it. It must be real.

Dalton walked to the entrance of Eskov and scanned Derek's access card. The entrance opened to them, and they walked inside.

Myha pointed the scrambler at the monitor in the corner.

Eskov was a skeleton crew at night. Only a few workers. As Director, Derek got to work when he wanted to. He was working days. Dalton wondered if Ayden would go home and tell him everything.

"We have to hurry," said Dalton.

"The blueprint shows the MCG is down in the center of the building," said Glenn. "We'll split up from here."

One bag had enough dynamite to power down the generator. The plan was to split up so if one team didn't make it, the other would. A third team would serve as a distraction. It didn't matter anyway because once the power was down, that was it. Everyone would have more important things to worry about.

"Here," said Myha, tossing Dalton one of the scramblers. "You'll need this."

Myha went with Jareth and his team. Glenn stayed with Dalton.

"Alright, let's go," said Glenn.

Dalton and Glenn teamed up with Mike and Gill. Dalton had talked to them a few times. Mike was tall like Dalton. All Dalton knew about him was that he liked to grow his own plants in his apartment. He didn't trust the food in Sector 14. Gill was into hoverboard racing, which had made them fast friends. After meeting him, Dalton recalled seeing him on the courses. His hoverboard had amazing turn-style navigation. He had built and designed it himself. Dalton was glad to hear he wasn't the only one sifting for parts in the trash piles outside the city walls.

Footsteps sounded on the steel floor.

Dalton and his companions shrank back, hidden behind the steadily humming machines. Dalton watched the worker pass. The worker was drinking his energy drink and talking into his access card.

Once the worker had passed, Glenn waved for them to keep going. They crept down the hallway to the stairwell. Dalton pointed the remote scrambler at the monitor in the stairway. They walked down seven flights of stairs. Dalton scrambled the monitors between each flight.

Finally, they got to the third floor of the building. Machines lined the floor in intricate rows. But in the center of the room was the MCG. The MCG towered over the other generators.

The third floor opened to the two floors above, allowing adequate room for the height of the massive machine.

The MCG was wider than it was tall. It had thick, red piping going from one side of the machine to the other.

Dalton walked up to the machine and unpacked the dynamite.

"Hey!"

Dalton looked up in alarm.

Thunderous feet echoed through the large room. Several cops were approaching them with their Thermal Phasers raised.

"Step away from the explosives!"

Dalton took out his lighter. The flame flickered. He could light the fuse here. It might be close enough to the generator to knock it out. He could light it and try throwing it. Either way, unless he stepped back, he would be shot.

Everything around him went silent as he knelt there, the flickering light in his hand.

Then . . . everything went dark.

10

A glaring light met Dalton's eyes as he opened them. He felt cold steel beneath his hands. His right hand felt oddly numb. Fresh, white bandages wrapped around it. He clenched it a few times. No pain.

He sat up and looked around. He was in a bare room. The floors were tiled. The walls were white. Everything looked clean, hospital clean.

He had a piercing headache. He reached up to his head. A large bump rose beneath his hair. It was tender.

Dalton hopped off the metal table. He opened the door to the room and peered outside. Behind the door was a long, tiled hallway. He poked his head out. No one was there.

He stepped out of the room and wandered down the hall. The last thing he remembered, he blacked out in a room full of cops. He thought he would be in jail in Sector 13, but this didn't look like a prison.

Where am I? A hospital? Maybe they took me here to patch me up before taking me to Sector 13. But then, why wasn't I handcuffed to that table?

As he walked down the empty hallway, Dalton tried to ignore his headache and focus on his surroundings. He didn't want any surprises. There were no sounds—no talking, no footsteps other than his own light ones, not even the hum of machines.

He stopped at a clear glass enclosure.

What in the . . .

Dalton stared, his hand pressed to the glass. He went numb. No, it was more than numbness. It was like he didn't *have* a body anymore. He was just eyes staring at what lay beyond the glass.

Inside the glass enclosure were rows and rows of artificial wombs. The large, pink sacks pulsed and shifted as the life moved inside them.

"Aren't they beautiful?" A voice said from behind him.

Dalton jumped, suddenly aware he still had ears to hear, and fearful he had lost time standing there. Had it been seconds, minutes, hours? He turned his head.

"Hello, Dalton. Welcome to Sector X. I'm Dr. Malax Anderson."

Dalton raised an eyebrow.

"You recognize that name: Anderson. I gave you that name."

Dr. Anderson was an older man, possibly in his early fifties. He had just started to gray. He was tall and thin. He had his hands in the pockets of his lab coat. Though the lab coat was long, Dr. Anderson's arms were bent at an awkward angle.

Dr. Anderson glanced down at Dalton's bandaged hand before his eyes returned to the glass enclosure. "I stitched up the wound. A normal boy would have died of infection, maybe loss the hand."

"What am I doing here?" asked Dalton. His throat was dry, but he didn't realize that until his voice croaked out like he was straining to breathe.

Dalton was taller than average, but Dr. Anderson's long body was a head taller. His limbs were unusually long. Dalton wondered if his fingertips would reach his knees were they hanging freely.

"You're here because of me, Dalton. You're Development 596. Do you know why I created you?" Dr. Anderson's eyes remained on the pulsing wombs. "I wanted to make someone more capable, smarter, and stronger than any of us. Your DNA has been genetically edited with only the best that mankind has to offer. Some of your attributes go beyond even that."

Dalton noticed the chain around Dr. Anderson's neck. At the end of it was a key. He looked away and back at the artificial wombs. "I thought they called off these experiments."

"They're not experiments anymore. We have perfected them. We have been creating perfect human beings long after you were born. You were the first of my successes. I discovered just the right sequence that would produce a fully functioning genetically enhanced person. The *discontinuation* of the project has only served us. Now artificial births are no longer required to be registered. So many of your younger brothers and sisters walk among you unknown."

My brothers and sisters? The only other Test-Tube Babies Dalton had ever met were either missing important body parts or left drooling in their chairs. "This is unethical," said Dalton. "Why are you showing me this?"

"If there is anyone who can survive in this city, it's beings like you, Dalton. You are the future, and you are the first. The conditions of this world might cause others to fall sick or to die, but not you. So, why fight it?"

Dalton stared at the movements of the wombs. He couldn't imagine it: Test-Tube Babies living like regular people, not shunned or looked down on. They would be adopted like normal children. They wouldn't have to spend their childhoods living in the Community House. They would have parents and, when they grew up, real jobs that earned enough that they wouldn't have to live in roach infested apartments.

"They're like me?" He knew they weren't *like* him. Only in a way. Dalton was abled-bodied and intelligent, but anyone who saw his identification code thought he was defective in some way. These artificial births—they would lead better, happier lives under the radar without a brand on their backs.

"Yes." Dr. Anderson approached the glass enclosure. "I've been keeping my eye on you, Dalton. You have excelled. It's time you were given a new access card." He handed Dalton the card. The numbers 596 at the end of his identification code had been removed.

"Your funds have been transferred," said Dr. Anderson. "Along with your contacts and any other data that was on the card. Now, you can really apply yourself. Get a new job, work your way up to the Assembly. There's no limit to what *you* can accomplish."

All his contacts . . . Dalton was happy he hadn't put Glenn or Myha onto his contact list. Dr. Anderson was probably having every one of his contacts looked into. "Why are you doing this for me?"

"I'd like to think of you as a son, Dalton. After all, your success is my success."

Dalton had the urge to cringe, but was careful not to. He looked down at the access card. "Thanks." He pocketed the card.

"There's an elevator down the hall. You can take it up to ground level."

Dalton took one last look at the artificial wombs. He didn't want to seem too eager to get out of there. Then, he walked away. He turned back, almost expecting Dr. Anderson to look back at him with his piercing eyes, but the doctor continued to gaze upon his newest creations with his hands clasped behind his back and the shadow of a smile upon his lips.

Dalton found his feet carrying him faster as he wandered down the hallway towards the elevator. The hall seemed longer than he imagined. The elevator had been like a pixel on a screen. It seemed to move further away the more steps he took towards it.

Finally, he reached it and punched the elevator button until the doors opened. Only two buttons labeled one and two ran along the metal panel. Dalton pushed one and waited as the elevator rose to ground level.

The doors opened. It was a sector Dalton had never been in before. Steel layered the floors and walls of the hallway where the elevator had taken him. Dalton turned the corner.

In a ballroom were tables of richly dressed people being served by waiters. They talked and laughed with a delicate air.

Dalton decided he didn't belong there. He wandered further down the hall until he found an airlock to the Safe Way. A few people stood in the large lobby in front of the exit. Without looking at anyone, Dalton pushed the button and was greeted by the hiss of air being released. He stepped inside as the door closed behind him and left through the second door into the Safe Way.

I'm being watched, he thought. Which means I shouldn't go to Myha and Glenn. I can't go back to my apartment either. They probably have the place bugged. I'd have to get rid of everything and tear out the cabinets and the walls too. If I started tearing up my apartment, that would look suspicious. But I don't like the idea of them watching me either.

He thought about Ayden's place. No, I can't go there, he thought. Ayden might have told Derek about us. Hell, Ayden could have turned us in. Those cops got there fast. No, Ayden wouldn't do that.

There was one place he'd decided he could go, but he really didn't want to go there.

He took the Shuttle to Sector 6. He opened the door to his apartment and looked around the room. Everything seemed to be the way he left it, but they would have been careful. They wouldn't want him to know they had planted something there.

Dalton grabbed a bag and shoved some clothes inside. He wrapped his hoverboard in a bedsheet and tucked it under his arm.

He boarded the Air Shuttle and got off at Sector 3. He walked along the Safe Way to the elevator and took the elevator to the top floor.

Apartment 1536.

Dalton rang the doorbell and waited.

She was dressed in a skin-tight shirt with a flowy, shimmering skirt. Her blonde hair was brushed pin straight.

"Well, if it isn't Dalton Anderson," said Giana.

I was born in the TRO system to two loving mothers. They raised me as any child in the TRO system would be raised: to respect all life and education. I guess they didn't think my childhood interest in humans would grow into something others would deem unnatural.

But I didn't care.

All through school I was bullied. My professors started discouraging me from focusing on human civilization as the topic for my class projects.

It didn't get better as I grew into an adult. At the simulation parties, I would always choose the human simulation. How I did like my human form.

I would always find a mirror in a dirty motel and gaze at it for hours.

My mothers eventually had what you would call *an intervention*. They sat down with me and impressed upon me that my obsession was unhealthy.

I begged them to let me go to Earth to observe the humans as we had for hundreds of thousands of years. Once I see a human, I told them, maybe I would no longer have this fascination with them.

No, they had said, trips to Earth were expensive and required extensive training. Besides, they didn't think it would work. If anything, it might increase my fascination.

My room was littered with catalogues of human entertainment, history, and languages. One day my mothers went into my room when I was gone, and threw out everything, every stitch of human related material. Gone.

When I returned, I was a wreck. I swore I would leave for good, and that's what I did. I wasn't there when my mothers decided to go to the REN system, where we go to die. They make the passing easy by injecting you with medicine that helps you move on. Our deaths can be quite painful, and we don't pass out from pain as some humans do. We suffer the full extent of it. It also makes the passing less gruesome for relatives as our skin starts to bubble instantly and foul odor fills the room in a matter of seconds. Better to let the professionals handle it, I guess.

I'm sorry to say that I wasn't there to say goodbye before my mothers' passing. That's not usually a problem for my kind, but I wanted to be there. I've seen enough of your art to know that *you* can understand that.

I blamed my obsession with humans on my inability to be there for my mothers before they died.

For five decades, I let go of that obsession, and started focusing on other life forms. I volunteered on the Sollup planet, getting the life forms oriented to their new homes. I became well-versed in the Sollup language which was a simple system of guttural sounds. But the Sollup lacked a sophisticated culture. They didn't even have multiple cultures within one species nor did they ever merge multiple cultures as the humans had. The Sollup simply developed from one simple, unified culture. They had no art, no music.

But I tried to enjoy my time among them. I even made a few Sollup friends. I was fitting in well with Sollup society.

Until one day, they started signing up volunteers for a new mission. You were in trouble. The humans needed help. I had to sign up.

11

Dalton sat up in the soft bed. The room was a brilliant white with touches of gold. The sheets and pillows were cool to the touch. Dalton didn't want to get up.

Giana turned over in her sleep. The sheets were wrapped around her body, but her naked shoulders rose and fell.

Dalton eased out of bed. He didn't want to wake her.

"Dalton."

He felt her soft hand on his wrist.

"Come back to bed." Her voice was almost a whisper.

"I need to use the bathroom."

He heard her turn back over on the bed.

Dalton grabbed his shorts and put them on before ambling to the bathroom.

The light above the mirror glowed. He looked at his reflection in the glass and ran his hand through his hair so it wouldn't look so matted.

He studied his features. His nose and the way his eyes slanted downward ever so slightly reminded him of Dr. Anderson. *Did he use some of his DNA to make me? Of course that arrogant bastard did.* Dalton shook the thought from his head.

He hoped Giana had something to relieve his headache. He opened the medicine cabinet. Something came tumbling out and into the sink. He picked it up. It was a box. He turned it over in his hand. There was a woman with blonde hair on the box. *Sun-kissed Golden Blonde.*

Dalton put the box of hair dye back in the medicine cabinet and grabbed a bottle of painkillers. He popped one into his mouth and drank the water from the faucet. He recalled all the chemicals they had pumped into the water at the treatment plant, and he felt a little sick.

Without waking Giana again, he went to the kitchen. Giana's entire apartment was painted white with white furnishings. He was afraid if he sat down or touched anything, he would dirty it. He padded across the plush hallway rug to the cold tiles of the kitchen.

He wasn't sure if the cereal Giana bought needed to be cooked or not. He poured it into a bowl and sat at the barstool to eat.

As he ate, he stared into the holograph painting that was meant to resemble a window looking out to an ocean.

Something mythical in UTC. Light was coming over the horizon. The night before, the painting had depicted a dark sky with tiny pinpoints of light.

Giana walked into the room. She wore a short nightgown that showed off her legs. Her footfalls were so soft, Dalton might not have noticed her walking in if he hadn't seen her out of the corner of his eye.

She approached him and planted a kiss on his cheek. Her blonde hair caressed the side of his face. "You didn't wait for me."

"Sorry. I was starving."

Giana got a bowl from the cabinet. "Did you have to bring that thing with you?" She was looking at his hoverboard leaning against the wall beside the front door. "Couldn't you have just left it at your apartment?"

Dalton shook his head. "Been having a major cockroach problem."

"Ew." Giana poured the cereal into a pot on the stove. "Just have Sector Maintenance handle it."

"There is no Sector Maintenance in Sector 6."

"You live in Sector 6." The corners of her lips turned downward like she had smelled something bad. "How come you never told me that?"

Dalton shrugged. "You never asked." It *was* true that she never asked, but that wasn't the reason he had kept it from her. He found himself not caring if he impressed her anymore. He shook his head. He rinsed his bowl in the sink. He walked back down the hallway.

He spotted his bag, discarded on the floor. He pulled out a clean shirt and some pants and put them on. Then, he shouldered his bag and walked back to the living room.

Giana was stirring her cereal at the stove. "Hey, where are you going?"

"I have to go back."

"Back? To your place?"

Dalton shook his head. He walked over to her. "I'm going to leave the city. You should go with me."

"Leave the city? What do you mean?"

Dalton gulped. "There's a way out of here. We can go to a place that looks like that." He pointed to the picture on the wall, the one masquerading as a window overlooking a beautiful seascape.

"Are you crazy, Dalton? We can't go out there. It was all destroyed years ago."

"No, it wasn't."

Giana folded her arms. "Dalton, did you take something?"

"I gotta go." Dalton grabbed his hoverboard.

"Hey, you can't just come in here and then leave like that. I'm not some doormat."

Dalton pressed the button on the side of the door, and the door slid open. He walked down the hall.

Giana shouted from the door. "If you leave like this, don't bother coming back! I did you a favor. You'll never get another girl like me! You think a girl would look twice if she knew what you really are?"

Something hit the wall as Dalton turned the corner. He figured Giana threw something. There was force there, but luckily, she wasn't a good aim.

*　*　*

Soft, solemn music fell on the worn chairs and across the stained walls.

Dalton approached the stage where Glenn was playing. The other crew members talked amongst themselves. The crew seemed smaller than they were before. *The others must have been taken in when we were busted.* Dalton glanced from one to another. His palms shook. He didn't see Myha.

As Dalton got closer, the talking stopped. Glenn's hands paused in mid-note, his fingers glancing off the keyboard.

"Dalton?"

Dalton hopped up onto the stage.

Myha came out from the back of the stage. She smiled when she saw Dalton.

Glenn stood from the piano. He clapped Dalton on the shoulder. "We thought we lost you. When I hit you—"

"*You* hit me?"

Glenn smiled. "Yeah. Sorry. You were just sitting there with that lighter in your hand. I thought they were going to shoot you. I was shouting at you, but you wouldn't respond. It was like you were in some sort of trance or something. I saw a crowbar.

I figured they wouldn't shoot you if you were passed out. So, I hummed it at your head."

"So, I have you to thank for this headache."

"How did you get out?" Myha stepped up to Dalton.

"They took me to this Sector. I saw an underground lab. I met this doctor who told me where I came from. He let me go."

Myha raised an eyebrow.

"You need to get outta here," said Dalton. "They don't care about you. They're building a breed of super humans who will be able to survive these conditions. We might as well just go. Let them have the city."

"We can't get through the door without the other key," said Myha.

"We'll blast it open," said Dalton. "We'll get more dynamite, and we'll blast the thing open."

Glenn shook his head. "We can't leave these people here."

"These people don't want to leave!" Dalton sighed.

"We know what's going on here." Glenn put his hand on his shoulder. "Doesn't that make us responsible?"

Dalton heard the airlock releasing. Everyone turned to the door.

Cops stormed into the building. They pointed their Phasers towards the stage and started shooting. Dalton threw himself to the floor.

"Glenn!"

Glenn staggered back as lasers penetrated his body. Sprays of blood painted the piano behind him. The keys of the piano sounded as Glenn's palm hit them. He fell against the side of the piano. His body shuttered to the floor.

Myha's voice echoed in Dalton's head. "No!" She was at Glenn's side, but his eyes were glassy and staring up. The way his eyes were wide, the way his mouth held that awed expression, it looked like he had seen something amazing.

Dalton pushed himself up from the ground. He felt like he was moving in slow motion.

Myha was crying. She held the necklace and the key that had been around Glenn's neck. Dalton grabbed her hand and led her behind the stage.

It was dark now. The cops had shot the lights on the stage. Jareth was shouting in a muffled, slow voice.

Dalton gripped Myha's hand.

Behind the stage was an airlock. Jareth was leading some of the crew through it. "Come on!" he shouted.

Thunderous feet were heading down the steps back stage.

Dalton put on his air mask and helped Myha put on hers. He went through the airlock. The air, thick and suffocating, dusted around them. Dalton took his hoverboard from his back.

"Stand here," he directed Myha. Dalton positioned himself at the front so he could control the speed. "Hold onto me and press down on the switch when I say so."

Myha put her arms around Dalton's waist.

"Now!"

She pressed down on the back switch, and they zoomed ahead.

Dalton pushed down in front, and the hoverboard picked up speed. The debris churned like dust behind them as they rode towards the outskirts of the city.

Myha shook Dalton's arm. "Stop!" Her scream was muffled by her air mask.

Dalton slowed his hoverboard to a halt.

Tears streamed down Myha's face. "Did they plant anything on you?"

He had showered the night before at Giana's place. But what if they put something under my skin, like Myha's parents did to her? Dalton's skin crawled.

"Did they give you anything?" Myha yelled through her mask.

Dalton's eyes went wide.

The access card.

He reached into his pocket and retrieved the card. "This."

Myha threw the card on the ground and stomped it with her boot. She stomped it again and again. The card was cracked into pieces. Myha was breathing heavy, and she was still stomping the tiny fragments.

12

Dalton took her by the arms. "Myha, stop!"

She was sobbing. "You led them right to us."

How could I have been so stupid? he thought. "I know. I'm sorry."

The hum of a hoverboard was getting louder. Jareth zoomed up to them. Shrink was on the back of his hoverboard.

Myha wiped her tears on the sleeve of her jacket. "How many got out?"

Jareth shook his head. "They followed us through the airlock. I grabbed Shrink here, and we got outta there. Gill, Rick, Jimmy, they never came to the back door. Pete and Cole ran when the cops came outside. They shot everyone else."

Myha hung her head. "We need to blow it up, the whole thing," she said through gritted teeth.

"We can't wait around for them to find us," said Jareth. "I know someplace we might be able to lie low for a while."

*   *   *

They entered Grim's warehouse. Chad sat behind the work counter. He was screwing in the back panel on a hoverboard. The light from the fluorescents beamed off the young boy's bald head.

"What do you want?" Chad must have sensed their presence because he didn't look up from his work.

"We need a place to hold up for a while." Jareth put his access card on the table. "We can pay."

"Grim!" Chad called over his shoulder. Then, he went back to his work.

"What is it, boy?" Grim came ambling out from the back.

"Jareth wants to know if he can shack up with us." Chad examined the tiny screw and realized it was stripped. He tossed it aside and picked up another one, which he carefully examined before screwing it into the hoverboard.

Dalton marveled at how well designed it was. He wondered if the boy designed it himself.

"I can pay," said Jareth.

"You better." Grim took Jareth's access card and handed it to Chad. "Charge him five thousand."

Five thousand! But the number didn't seem to faze Jareth.

"Come on." Grim waved. "I have a few cots. They're not the most comfortable, but they should do."

* * *

Grim warmed cans of food on an iron skillet over the fire pit. He wrapped each can in a thick towel and passed them around.

"What is this?" asked Shrink.

"Do I come into your house and ask your momma about *her* fine cooking?" One corner of Grim's lips tightened. "I don't eat that stuff they grow in a lab. They put chemicals in it, chemicals that make you think different, chemicals that make you think that the only things that are important are new devices, new filters, and that damned Mega Screen. Luckily, I found stockpiles of canned food. I've been eating it almost all my life now. I don't give a damn about the Mega Screen." He passed a can to Chad, who took it in silence.

They all sat around the fire pit on large metal canisters. The canister that Grim sat on was dwarfed by his massive body. Chad was a bird beside him perched in his seat. They were a ridiculous pair.

Dalton put his hand up to his mouth to hide the smile that had spread on his face. He shouldn't be smiling. Glenn was dead, and he was smiling. Of course, Dalton had never properly mourned for anyone in his life—he hadn't had anyone to mourn for.

Dalton propped his lid up with his spoon. He had a can of beans. It smelled sweet. He dug his spoon into the can and ate.

It wasn't bad. It wasn't good either. It left his mouth feeling dry. He took a swig of the drink. That didn't make it better.

Myha wasn't eating. "We need more dynamite."

Chad looked up from his food.

"Why?" Grim asked, half-chewing.

They were silent.

Chad stared at her. "Tell us why you need it this time, or we won't sell it to you."

"We're blowing up Eskov."

Grim spit, spraying his food across the room.

Chad's expression didn't change.

"You wanna do what?" Grim put his hand on his knee.

"We're *going* to blow up Eskov." Myha's expression didn't change either.

"That's where all the city's power comes from!" Grim said it like he was explaining it to a child.

"You said you didn't like the Mega Screen," said Myha.

"Yeah, but I *do* like living," said Grim. "You shut the power off and everything in the city goes down, including the towers. I have enough food and water to last a lifetime, but fresh air . . . that's a commodity I can't do without."

Myha stood. She pressed down on her palm. The map glowed in front of them. Myha waited for the instructions to load above the map.

Grim squinted to read them. "Where'd you get that?"

"You won't be breathing fresh air for much longer. This city is going to shit," said Myha. "I don't want to be here when it does, do you? I'm the only one who has this map. So, we either do things my way, or we all get to die here."

Dalton wasn't sure what it was: that look in Myha's eyes of total and utter sincerity, the way a map just sprang from the palm of her hand, or the fact that Grim had been on the outside of things for so long.

"Okay," said Grim. "We'll get you the dynamite."

"With that much dynamite," Chad shuffled in his seat, "you'll need someone experienced to help plant it. And you'll need a hovercar."

"Where are we going to get one of those?" asked Shrink. "They've been banned for years."

Hovercars were banned because they caused too much pollution. The Assembly decided that hovercars were overtaxing the city filters. They didn't look to the televisions, computers, or the Mega Screen that was sucking massive amounts of energy. But those things couldn't be shut down. They were necessary to spread the Assembly's propaganda.

Chad got up from his seat and walked out the doorway. When the others didn't follow, he poked his head back in. "What? You don't think I'm bringing it in here to show you."

Jareth got up from his seat in a rush, abandoning his can there. Shrink put his can on the ground and joined them followed by Myha and Dalton. Grim didn't move from his spot and continued to eat his food. Dalton caught him glancing at Chad's can before following the others through the door.

They followed Chad to a large back room. At the end of the room was a giant airlock, ten feet high and twenty feet wide. Chad switched on the lights.

There wasn't just one hovercar. There were two rows of hovercars, eight cars total.

"Grim salvaged the parts, and I fixed 'em up. It's been a hobby of mine. Never did get to take one out for a ride.

"We could pack enough dynamite in two cars," said Chad.

Dalton ran his hand along the side of one of the hovercars. *Amazing*.

* * *

Dalton stared straight ahead. Not only was this his first time driving a hovercar, it was also his first time driving a hovercar packed with dynamite.

Sweat formed on Dalton's brow. He wiped it away on his sleeve.

Jareth was driving fast in front of him, darting between buildings and debris piles. Shrink was in Dalton's passenger seat. Myha and Chad were with Jareth.

They halted at the first floor of the Eskov building. Many of the buildings were abandoned at the ground level because of the thick cloud of debris. Newer buildings were filled with cement up to the third floor. The filters were not as efficient the closer the floor was to ground level.

They focused the headlights of their hovercars on the building.

Dalton put on his air mask.

Chad got out of the back of the car Jareth was driving. He approached Dalton's car right as Dalton was getting out. "I need you both to carefully place the dynamite around the perimeter of the building. I'm going to find a way inside. If you want this building to fall, we need to place the dynamite strategically. You must be careful. Some of this dynamite Grim's been stockpiling, it's very old."

Dalton started unloading his car. He strapped his hoverboard onto his back just in case. He began placing the dynamite along the sides of the building, careful not to tangle the long fuse. Jareth, Myha, and Shrink were also planting the explosives along the building.

There was sweat on his brow, but Dalton couldn't wipe it away beneath the mask.

Blasts rang out in the distance. *Were those Phasers?*

Chad came running from behind the building. "We have to get out of here. They're coming."

Jareth and Shrink dropped what they were doing and followed Chad to the hovercar. Dalton was next to Myha. "Come on, Myha, let's get out of here."

Dalton couldn't see her eyes behind her goggles.

Myha ducked her head and ran to the fuse. She flickered the lighter, but the light kept going out. Dalton ran to where Myha was crouched.

"What are you doing?" Jareth yelled from the car.

"Myha, let's go," said Dalton, taking her arm, but she shrugged him away.

The engine from Jareth's car revved.

Lasers were hitting the building.

Myha kept trying to get the lighter to work. Finally, the lighter stayed lit long enough for her to light the fuse.

A blast hit the building, and suddenly, there was an explosion.

Dalton grabbed Myha and tried to run from the blast, but he was too late. They were thrown to the ground and landed several feet away from where they had stood.

Dalton turned around on his side. He could see the spark in the distance. The fire was dancing up the fuse line.

"Myha!"

She was lying face down.

Dalton got up on his hands and knees. There was a ringing in his ears, but he could hear the blasts from the Phasers like he was underwater.

The hovercar was a distance away. Its headlights had been blown out.

I don't know if it still works, but it's too far away to take the chance. Dalton pulled his hoverboard off his back. He picked Myha up from the ground and slung her body over his shoulder.

Dalton pressed the button on the back of his hoverboard and turned it up to full speed. He blasted away just in time. A loud series of short, flat bangs caused Dalton's ears to pop. Then, he heard the loudest sound he had ever heard in his entire life: the roar of the Eskov building coming down.

Dalton was tempted to turn his head to see its collapse, but with Myha's extra weight, he had to concentrate on staying balanced and maneuvering the hoverboard at maximum speed.

Smoke and debris rushed forward from behind him, making it difficult to see in the already cloudy atmosphere. In front of him, the lights of the buildings and the Safe Ways were going out in a massive wave. All before the dust had even settled.

Big chunks of debris rained down from the falling building.

Dalton dodged them as they littered his path. Something metal, possibly a smaller generator shuttered to the ground, missing him by a mere few feet.

The buildings and the Mega Screen went dark. Dalton struggled to see. The beams on his hoverboard glowed, but did not supply adequate light.

Dalton felt heat at his back and was acutely aware of the taste in his mouth. *Blood?* He hoped the blast hadn't knocked any teeth out when it hit him. His arm tingled.

I just have to keep going, he thought. *I can't let that building come down on us.* He wasn't sure exactly how far away from the crumbling mass he needed to be. He felt like he was going in slow motion, but his hoverboard couldn't carry them any faster.

Sweat was getting into his eyes and dripping down to his lips. He tried to ignore the tickling as he sped through the city.

Myha's weight was shifting. *She's waking up. Good.*

A pane of glass jetted into the ground in front of him. Dalton turned the hoverboard sharply, avoiding it.

As he zoomed along, the dust stopped churning, and the projectiles became fewer. Dalton slowed his hoverboard.

"Dalton Anderson!" A voice boomed.

Dalton turned, falling back from his hoverboard. He hit the ground with a thud.

The Mega Screen was glaring in the distance. The shadowed silhouettes of four men in lab coats appeared on the screen.

What the . . .?

Dalton stared at the screen. His eyes wide.

The lights of the Safe Ways blinked back on.

But Eskov was a crumbling mass on the ground. Even the Safe Way that connected it to the Shuttle area had been torn away. But the lights were coming back *on*.

You gotta be shitting me.

The camera was focusing in on the doctors, bringing them closer into frame. But their faces were hidden in the backlit room. Then, suddenly, the screen went orange. It turned the whole city amber.

Myha groaned across Dalton's shoulder.

"Myha?" Dalton lifted her from his shoulder and helped her to sit up.

Her eyes blinked open. She brought her hand up to her head. "Uh. What happened?"

"Eskov went down, but the lights came back on. The city must have backup generators or something."

"Everything's in Eskov. If the city had other backups why wouldn't we know about them?"

"Stuff like this," he said, motioning to where Eskov had fallen.

"We have to find those generators."

"No, it's over. They're going to hunt us down and make sure we never tell anybody anything."

13

Leanne's face was on the screen. "Last night a group of terrorists blew up the Eskov building. Fortunately, city officials were able to get the power back on via a secret system of generators, the location of which cannot be disclosed. Sources indicate that among the individuals responsible for this attack of terrorism is one Dalton Anderson."

The picture from Dalton's access card was projected on the screen.

"Also responsible for the attack are the following individuals. Images of Myha, Jareth, Shrink and Gill were featured. "The identity of these individuals is unknown. If you have any information about these criminals, please call 999."

Dalton and Jareth sat in front of Shrink's computer.

Grim was cutting the end of a wire. "Well, you're wanted men now. You'll need new access cards and new faces. I know someone who can work wonders. That is if the tissues take."

Jareth shook his head. "We should have known they had backups."

"At least we know Gill is alive," said Shrink.

"Yeah, but for how long?" asked Jareth. "Grim's right. We can't show our faces in the city now. Eventually, they're gonna track us down."

"Then we can't be in the city." Dalton was cleaning the filters of his air mask.

"You're as crazy as Glenn was," said Jareth, "and you saw where that got him."

"Glenn put others before himself. He was a good person, that's what got him killed. I'm talking about putting ourselves before everyone else. I'm talking about getting out of here."

Grim shook his head. "Go talk crazy somewhere else." He ambled out of the room.

Dalton set down his air mask. He didn't want to become someone different just so he would be able to sleep at night.

"I can afford to get us all new faces," said Jareth.

"How is that exactly?" asked Dalton.

Jareth folded his arms. "You didn't know? My father is on the Assembly. I ran away when I was thirteen, but every year, he sends money to my access card. He probably doesn't know what I look like anymore, but if he sees my photo on the news, he might remember me. That means no more money, I guess. But I still have enough for all of us to get the operation."

Dalton stood. "I don't want to change my face because you're too afraid to get out of here."

"What does it matter?" Jareth shouted as Dalton left the room. "You scarred up that face anyway!"

* * *

Dalton held two cups of coffee.

On the counter, Myha sat, projecting the map in front of her.

Dalton handed Myha a cup, and the map swept across the room.

She took a sip and put the cup down on the counter. She lifted her palm up and gazed at the map. "When I was little, when I was alone, I would shine this thing and stare at it for hours. My dad used to say the world was beautiful once. It wasn't always hard and metal and cold."

Her eyes glistened. "These are my parents." She opened her locket, and the faces of her parents projected above the metal enclosure. "I thought maybe I could make a difference. Finish where they left off, you know. But, they never told me what they wanted me to do with this map. They've been gone for years, but right now, I've never felt so alone."

Dalton swept over the smooth skin of her face and cradled her chin. He pulled her in, but stopped just as his lips brushed hers.

"I have to go." Dalton whispered against her lips.

When he pulled away from her, her eyes were open, her lips parted. "Go? Where?"

"I have to turn myself in."

"Turn yourself in? No. What are you talking about?" She backed away from him and looked him in the eyes.

"I know where the second key is. It's around Malax Anderson's neck. I'm going to get it."

"You're going back to Sector X?"

Dalton nodded. "There are some things I'm going to need you to do for me. The others will think it's crazy—"

"*I* think it's crazy."

He took her hands in his. "I need you to convince them to leave, to follow the map and go down to the tunnels. You'll meet me there after I have the key."

She shook her head. "No. We'll blow open the exit, like you said."

"That door was designed to withstand maximum impact. Just like the dome is resistant to explosives, that door is too. We need the key. Here's my old access card. Tell Jareth there are air tanks in Sector 11. We'll need them. If I don't show up in twenty-four hours, I've failed."

"We've done everything we can, Dalt."

"Not yet. There's one last thing we need." Dalton took her hand, the one from which the map projected. He rubbed over the surface of her skin where the chip was. "We need to get this thing out. We need to show it to everyone."

Myha paused. Her eyes searched his. Then, she nodded. She flattened her palm.

Dalton reached into his pocket and pulled out his knife. Snapping it open, he pressed the blade against her palm and etched around the chip.

Myha didn't look away as blood pooled over the edges of her hand.

He took the chip out. It was small, the diameter of a bottle cap. Dalton rubbed its flat surface between his fingers. When he clicked it, the map was projected in front of him.

Myha laughed. "It's been in my hand so long, it's weird seeing it on the outside."

Blood was dripping from her hand.

Dalton grabbed the towel from the counter and pressed it into her palm.

Myha winced.

"Sorry," he said.

"It's fine," she said. "I'll deal with it. You go. Get us out of here."

* * *

Shrink was at his computer. He was playing a game. Probably trying to get his mind off the news broadcast they had just watched.

"Shrink." Dalton approached him. "I need you to do something for me."

Shrink swiveled around in his chair. "What's that?"

Dalton held up the chip. "This is Myha's map. Would you be able to hack into the Mega Screen and project this?"

"I could do that."

* * *

Dalton took a deep breath and pushed the second button on the elevator. He knelt to the ground as security rushed him. They had on masks. Gas flooded the hallway.

Dalton felt light-headed and dizzy. He collapsed on the floor.

"Dalton Anderson."

Dr. Malax Anderson's blurred image came into focus. He had a needle in his hand.

Dalton's arms and legs were restrained. He was upright on an X-shaped table. Cuffs had been wrapped around his wrists and ankles.

They had taken Dalton's clothes and dressed him in a white shirt and pants, like hospital scrubs.

"You're playing a dangerous game, Dalton. I gave you a chance to redeem yourself, and you wasted it."

"Why are you afraid of us getting out?"

"Afraid of you getting out? There's nothing out there, Dalton. And even if there was, it doesn't matter. You're better than the rest. Can't you see that? You can live in this city into old age with no fear of the air outside its buildings. So, there will be no need for Safe Ways or air filters. You were built to sustain. You think the world as it once was would have allowed such progress? Let me tell you about the world you dream of.

Real science, real improvements, are regulated and suppressed. Money is more important than science. Cures are ignored because treatment brings in more revenue. Work like mine, work that makes us better, would be criticized and challenged."

"Your work *was* challenged. That's why you built this underground lab to hide it."

Dr. Anderson shook his head. "The public challenged my work. The Assembly didn't. How do you think I was able to build this lab? The Assembly still funds me. They want the same thing I do. The same thing you should want. You are the future, Dalton Anderson. You should have learned to embrace that."

Dr. Anderson walked around him.

Dalton felt the needle invade the base of his neck. "What are you doing?" Dalton asked through clenched teeth.

"Extracting your cerebral fluid," said Dr. Anderson. "Since you aren't putting it to good use, I could use it for your new brothers and sisters."

Dalton felt something cold drip down his neck as the needle left his body.

"There." Dr. Anderson placed the fluid filled needle down. He pressed a button on the side of the table, and after a few seconds, two men in white scrubs entered the room.

"Take him to Room 5 and make sure he is well secured." Dr. Anderson looked away from Dalton and back to the table.

The orderlies unstrapped the cuffs that bound Dalton's hands and feet. They lowered his body from the table.

Dalton wrenched his arm from the first orderly and elbowed him in the face. He slammed his fist into the jaw of the second orderly, knocking him to the ground.

Dr. Anderson turned. He held a needle. He threw his body on top of Dalton. The needle was inches from Dalton's face.

Dalton grabbed Dr. Anderson's arm, trying to stop him from plunging the needle into him.

"Hold him down!" Dr. Anderson shouted.

The orderlies scrambled to their feet, but they didn't rush to Dr. Anderson's aid.

Suddenly, debris filled air started to come into the room from the air vents.

"Why are you just standing there? Help me!" Dr. Anderson was struggling on top of Dalton.

The orderlies ran from the room as the air rushed in. Dr. Anderson looked around as the thick air surrounded them. "What did you do?"

I knew it. Tower 8. It filters the air for Sector X. It was the only tower unaccounted for. Dalton had ripped the filters from the tower before coming to the underground. It was only a matter of time before the building's internal filters would give out.

Dalton clenched the key and ripped the necklace off Dr. Anderson's neck.

Dr. Anderson was coughing. He crawled off Dalton.

Dalton scrambled to his feet and ran to the door. His hand was clasped across his mouth and nose. He ran down the hallway in the direction he thought the room with the door might be.

He turned the corner and went down the adjoining corridor. Polluted air leaked into the hallway. Dalton was afraid to lift his hand from his nose and mouth.

He heard someone behind him.

Dalton turned his head.

There, staring at him from the opposite end of the hallway, was a man in a bulky, out-of-date gas mask. *Dr. Anderson.* Swinging his arms, he ran towards Dalton. In his hand was a Phaser.

Dalton slammed his hand against the button on the side of the door at the end of the hallway. He walked inside and closed the door just as a laser zipped from down the hall.

The air was worse in here.

A ladder led up to the door. Dalton ran to it. He pulled his shirt up over his nose and mouth and climbed.

The door burst open.

A laser zinged against the metal ladder.

Dalton ducked. His shirt fell back to his neck. Dalton couldn't hold his breath anymore. He breathed in the bad air, but he didn't choke. He didn't cough.

He made it to the top of the ladder, to the platform with the door.

Dalton ducked as the laser zinged. Sparks showered down on him.

There *was* a keyhole in the door. Dalton put the key into the lock and turned it. The door opened.

I was right!

A laser shot hit his arm. Dalton screamed.

Opening the door, he rushed inside. He jammed the key into the lock and turned it. Leaning against the door, he breathed in the air. He covered his mouth. He wasn't sure how long he could breathe it in.

14

Dalton climbed down the ladder into the tunnel. It was dark except for the light from the window of the door above. *They must have closed up the tunnel where I fell in.*

He felt his way down the tunnel until his hands lighted upon jagged rocks. *The rocks that were blocking the other side.* He thought Ran-Ran had said city officials had it cleared, but they only covered it up.

Dalton started pulling rocks away with his bare hands. Dr. Anderson must have taken Dalton's gloves off. His bandage was still secure, however. Smaller fragments of rock cascaded to his feet. Dalton backed away until he could no longer hear the rocks tumbling down.

He felt around the rock pile. *There!* A space between the pile and the wall. He stepped forward, leaning as close as he could to the wall of the tunnel. A jagged piece of rock bit through the cloth of his shirt, leaving a long cut across his chest. He tried to ignore it. He was more than half way through.

Finally, he ambled out to the other side. In the distance, lights blinked. He looked up. Florescent lights lined the top of the tunnel. However, the bulbs had gone dark. *The lights up ahead must be the same. These lights were probably damaged when the ground fell in.*

He wasn't sure how they were connected to the city's power. He looked back. He hadn't noticed any lights on the other side of the tunnel. But they could have gone out as well.

Dalton wandered down the tunnel. Water soaked his cloth slippers.

"Hello?" Dalton shouted. His voice echoed down the tunnel.

Blood was running down his arm and chest. It was tickling his skin. He wished he had something to bandage up the wounds. The pain dulled to a numb throb.

Lights danced on the wall. A flashlight focused on Dalton's face.

"Dalt!" The flashlight moved away from his face, and someone rushed over to him. It was Myha. "What the hell happened to you?"

"I was Dr. Anderson's lab rat." Dalton said through his hand.

"You're not wearing an air mask!"

Myha grabbed an air mask and helped him put it on.

"Here's your stuff." Myha handed him his pocket knife and a flashlight. She removed his hoverboard from her back.

"Hey." Jareth had an air tank in both hands. "Thanks for the heads up about the tanks." He helped Dalton put the tank on his back.

Dalton hooked the air mask to the tank. "Thanks. I thought I was going to die in here."

"Did you get the key?" Jareth asked.

Dalton held the key up in his bloodied hand.

"Ha-ha!" Jareth clapped him on the back. "Let's get the hell out of here!"

Myha pushed down the chip and the map was projected between them. "That is the exit." She pointed to the glowing orange door. "That red dot there. I think that's us. I always noticed how it moved when I was a kid."

"Alright." Dalton turned on his flashlight.

Behind Myha and Jareth stood Shrink, Chad, and Grim. Myha did it. She got them here. Now it was up to Dalton to get them out.

More roaches crawled through the tunnel than in Dalton's apartment. *What were they eating? How could they live out here?* Dalton suddenly had an admiration for the creatures. They were strong, resilient. They could survive anything.

They made it to the blinking lights. Along the walls of the tunnel, curving down to the floor, were bright fluorescent lights.

They blinked in a wave down the tunnel. After two hours, the light above them glowed and went out followed by the next one and so on, journeying down the tunnel. The closer the red dot got to the exit, the faster the lights would start over again until the light above them glowed one hour after it had gone out.

They were nearing a side tunnel. It was dark. The lights would not come back around for at least another ten minutes if Dalton timed it right.

Something was crouching in the dark. Dalton shined his flashlight on it. Its pale skin was stretched across its body. The spine protruded from its back leading to its bald skull. Its long fingers waded in the water.

Dalton's eyes were wide. He swept the flashlight back down again.

"What was that?" whispered Myha.

Dalton shook his head.

Suddenly, the lights came back around and glowed on the monster.

It turned its head, staring right at Dalton. It leapt.

Dalton fell onto his back. He reached for the knife in his pocket. He slashed at the creature until its blood was dripping down his arm and onto his face and neck.

His own voice boomed from the Mega Screen. "If you are hearing this, then I and a few brave friends from United Trace Z3T have evacuated the city. The following is a list of guidelines that were left to us for the purpose of leaving UTC Z3T:

URGENT: GUIDELINES FOR EVACUATION

IF YOU ARE READING THIS, THE SENSORS LOCATED OUTSIDE UNITED TRACE Z3T HAVE DETECTED THAT THE LAND IS ONCE AGAIN HABITABLE. IT IS IMPERATIVE THAT YOU EXIT IMMEDIATELY AS UNITED TRACE Z3T WAS DESIGNED AS A TEMPORARY SAFE HOUSE AND IS NOT SUITABLE FOR LONG-TERM HABITATION.

He had asked Shrink to make it loud enough so people would hear it in their apartments. Shrink had done just that. It would play in a continuous loop. Right now, the people would be seeing the map projected on the Mega Screen, and the Assembly would be powerless to take it down.

Dalton scrambled to his feet.

A loud chorus of growling and the splashing of water echoed down the tunnels. Creatures were rounding the bend. Some were humanoid, perhaps animals mixed with human body parts and features or perhaps humans mixed with animal parts and features. Others looked like oversized hairless rats. Hundreds of these creatures were running towards them.

TWO ACCESS KEYS WILL ACTIVATE THE EXIT DOOR.

THE EXIT IS LOCATED IN THE CITY'S EXISTING SEWAGE TUNNELS. THERE ARE DESIGNATED DOORS TO THE TUNNELS LOCATED AT THE GLOWING POINTS ON THE MAP BELOW.

The water churned as Dalton and the others ran down the tunnel.

Is this what he did with them? Dalton wondered. For how many years had Dr. Anderson been chucking his discarded experiments through that door and into the tunnel? It would explain why the number of artificial births went up to six hundred with so many gaps in between. Some were entirely unfit for human society.

He kicked up the water as he ran. He looked over his shoulder.

Chad was lighting and throwing dynamite behind him, but the fuses kept hitting the water and going out before the dynamite exploded.

PROCEED THROUGH THESE DOORS AND INTO THE TUNNELS. THE EXIT IS INDICATED BY THE ORANGE SQUARE ON THE MAP.

PLACE THE ACCESS KEYS INTO THE LOCKING MECHANISM AND TURN EACH KEY TWO ROTATIONS CLOCKWISE.

"We have to get on our hoverboards!" Jareth was taking his hoverboard off his back.

Grim was falling behind. "I can't ride that thing. I'll never be able to maintain my balance." Grim stopped. He reached into his bag and pulled out some dynamite.

Chad turned around, his hoverboard in his hands. "Grim, you can ride on the back of mine."

"I'll never fit, my boy. Go."

Dalton looked back. Chad was still standing there, and the creatures were closing in.

"Go!" Grim shouted.

Chad threw down his hoverboard and got on.

Grim lit the dynamite. He touched the top of Chad's bald head.

That was the last thing Dalton saw before he threw his own hoverboard to the ground and got onto it. Myha got on behind him and put her arms around his waist. Jareth zoomed ahead of them with Shrink at his back.

The explosion sounded and the tunnel vibrated.

They were thrown forward. Dalton was jerked off his hoverboard. Body parts rained down on them.

EXIT IN AN ORDERLY FASHION.

15

Dalton got to his feet. The tunnel was dark where the explosion had gone off. Myha was up, helping Shrink to his feet.

Chad knelt in the water.

Jareth was against the wall with his hand on his air tank.

Dalton approached him and offered Jareth his hand. Jareth lifted his hand from his air tank. The air hissed out of it.

Dalton knelt beside him. "Does anyone have any tape?"

"No," said Myha. "Why?"

"I got a leak," Jareth said. "So, this is how I'm going to go down?"

"Do you have your filter mask?" asked Dalton.

"Ha." Jareth's laugh was muffled through his mask. "The pollution's too thick down here. What do we have? Another hour? Even if we ride our hoverboards the entire rest of the way, my filters will get full of junk. Then, I'm gone, Test-Tube. You might as well take my hoverboard and go on without me."

"You have enough air. You'll make it."

Jareth shook his head. "Most of the air leeched out before I noticed it. I got maybe ten, fifteen minutes of breathing left. It's fine. What are you worried about? It's not like I've been doing you any favors."

Dalton continued to kneel there. Jareth had done one really shitty thing to him, but if it wasn't for Jareth, he would be stuck in his roach infested apartment for the rest of his life.

"You know," said Jareth. "I convinced myself you were only able to beat me on the Slope because of your superpowers."

"Superpowers?"

"Yeah, the ones you have because you were born in a lab."

Dr. Anderson's words echoed in his head: You can live in this city into old age with no fear of the air outside its buildings. So, there will be no need for Safe Ways or air filters. You were built to sustain.

In a rush, Dalton disconnected his air tank from his mask and took the tank off his back.

"What are you doing?" asked Jareth.

"I don't need it." Dalton was taking the tank off Jareth's back.

"Are you crazy?"

Dalton ripped his mask off his face and took a deep breath. "See. I don't need it. You do."

Jareth allowed him to put the air tank on his back and connect it to his mask.

"Dalton." Myha walked up behind him.

He turned to face her. "It's okay. Let's get back on our hoverboards." He took a deep breath. "It's time everyone is able to do this again."

* * *

They zoomed through the tunnels on the hoverboards. Shrink rode on the back of Chad's. Jareth was at the head of the crew. They had been riding for nearly an hour and were covering a good bit of distance on the hoverboards.

A loud boom echoed through the tunnel.

Dalton turned around. Myha clung to him.

Another boom echoed.

She turned her head too.

A cement wall slammed shut in the tunnel behind them.

Dr. Anderson, Dalton thought. There must be some sort of safety mechanism to prevent anything dangerous from getting in.

Dalton increased the speed of the hoverboard. Jareth and Chad increased their speed as well. They zoomed through. The booming sound was getting closer.

The cement wall slammed right behind them. Dalton could feel the air it forced out when it went down. Myha tightened her grip on his waist. *She knows what I'm about to do.* He increased the speed on his hoverboard.

The boom sounded loud in Dalton's ears. There was a fork in the tunnel.

"Which way?" Jareth yelled.

Myha pressed down on the chip. "Left. Shit!"

"What?" Dalton asked.

"I dropped the map."

Dalton turned the hoverboard.

"No, Dalton, we can't go back for it. We won't make it."

He zoomed ahead. He could see the chip. The map was still projected above it.

"Dalton, no!"

Hoping to scoop it up, Dalton reached down into the water.

Myha pulled him back as the cement wall came crashing down on the chip. The map was gone.

Dalton turned the hoverboard back around and shot forward. *Without the map, we'll be wandering around aimlessly. Wait!* Dalton closed his eyes. He remembered the map. He remembered it exactly.

Pushing the hoverboard to maximum speed, he was able to catch up with Jareth and Chad.

"We have another turn up ahead," said Jareth. "Did you get the map?"

"No," said Dalton. "But I know where to go."

Dalton zipped ahead. The lights were coming back faster. Dalton turned bend after bend, remembering the map in detail. In less than ten minutes, they would make it to the exit. The cement block crashed down behind them.

There it was: the exit.

The door looked heavy. A light arched around its perimeter.

Dalton's hoverboard shuttered. It halted. Myha and Dalton were thrown from it and into the water.

"Jareth, wait!" Dalton yelled.

Jareth jolted to a stop in front of them.

Dalton ambled to his feet and helped Myha to hers. He guided her towards Jareth's hoverboard. Myha stepped up onto it.

"Dalton, get on!" Jareth shouted.

"You know there's no room."

"We're not leaving without you," said Myha.

"You need to go before that cement door shuts. I need you to get out of here." Dalton reached into his pocket, grabbed the key, and held it out to Jareth.

Jareth gripped Dalton's hand in his. He took the key. Then, he sped off with Myha.

Dalton picked up his hoverboard and ran. He kept his eyes focused on the door. Chad and Shrink had made it.

Dalton ran faster than he had ever ran in his life. He didn't pay attention to his breathing. He barely noticed the water splashing against his legs.

All the while, he was hitting the back of his hoverboard, hoping he could shake whatever was loose.

Glenn's song played in his head. It was blissful and sorrowful at the same time.

Suddenly, the hoverboard roared to life.

Dalton threw it to the ground and jumped on top of it, bringing the speed all the way up. He zoomed across the water towards the door.

The cement wall was starting to fall.

Dalton dropped his body as low as he possibly could, lying down on his hoverboard.

The wall crashed down.

Dalton tumbled into the water. He got to his knees.

Myha had her arms around him. His face was inches away from the cement wall. Jareth came over and clapped him on the shoulder.

Dalton ambled to his feet. There they were, at the exit. The light around the door blinked.

"You want to do the honors." Jareth held up the key Dalton had given him.

He took the key from Jareth and approached the door with Myha. Myha put her key in and turned it.

Dalton looked at the key in his hand. He took a deep breath and placed it into the lock. He wasn't sure what he would see, what the world would look like, but he imagined it would be open and green.

He pulled the door open, and brilliant light met his eyes. It was so bright, it was blinding.

CONGRATULATIONS UNITED TRACE Z3T. YOU SURVIVED AND CAN BEGIN TO REBUILD.

Z

Have you ever seen a flower bloom and die in a time lapse?
That was my entire experience of human culture. I was born the day it started, but it seemed to decay so quickly when I wasn't even half-way through my life.

We knew it would take us centuries to get to Earth.

It was the responsibility of the volunteers to expose ourselves to as much human culture as possible. Once again, I was surrounded by catalogues of Earth music, history, and art. The purpose of this was to orient ourselves to your customs and habits as to better communicate with and encourage you.

It's strange. Even my fellow volunteers, who were journeying to Earth for the sole purpose of saving humankind, thought my obsession with human culture and mannerisms was unnatural.

I thought that aboard the ship to Earth, I would finally be able to express my interests in humans to the fullest extent, but in fact it was quite the opposite.

My fellow volunteers saw me as a fanatic who only wanted to go to Earth to satisfy my own interest rather than the interest of the alien species we were going to Earth to protect. How ridiculous? Of course, I care about you. I missed my mothers' passing for you.

I took some of the catalogues and found a quiet place on the ship to spend the next hundred years. You see, I'm remarkably good at being alone. Every now and then, I slink out for food and then I would come back to my little cubbyhole away from the world.

It's ironic now my need for contact. At this point, I could even stand for someone pointing in my face and calling me strange. It's funny, loners, they think they could be alone forever and not be bothered by the lack of conversation, but they don't realize all the small moments when you're forced to make conversation out in the world. You might dread it at the time, but once you're really alone, you start to realize how beneficial it was.

But once we neared planet Earth, I ran from my hole at lightning speed. I had to see what I'd been waiting for. I knew it would not be as I had read, but the magnitude didn't hit me until I saw it.

The Sun was bright red. All the green had died. The oceans were starting to dry up. Perhaps if you hadn't been sheltered, it wouldn't have stifled your advancement. Perhaps you would have made it to another star system before your star had started to die.

Had we not saved you, in another five billion years or so, the expanding sun would have engulfed Earth, but you would have died long before that. Eventually, the sun's increasing heat would have penetrated your domed cities, killing all remaining life inside.

When we landed on the planet, I rushed out onto the barren land. It was dry and cracked. Steam was puffing in the air.

The plan wasn't to assist you unknowingly. But it was too dangerous to take you out of your protective environments. So, we did the next best thing.

I was exhausted on the trip home. I retired to my hole. There was no way of communicating with you. We had tried everything.

I woke to a great shuttering throughout the ship. My eager hands touched the windows. Plasma blasts were hitting the ship.

I knew it was the Chas.' You might refer to them as the Prometheans. They were responsible for your achievement. Like us, part of their DNA rests in you. We are cousins in that way. But the Prometheans never liked our endeavors to save other lifeforms, especially lifeforms that the Prometheans themselves created.

That might sound strange to you, but, you see, the Prometheans wanted their creations to live and die naturally. They liked watching how you developed. They wanted to make a progressive race, but where was the challenge if another lifeform always came to the rescue. They wanted you to learn to fend for yourselves.

They were angry at us for interrupting that. They were curious to see if you would have found a way out of your predicament. Although we hadn't technically helped, we were there. We had tainted it.

The Promethean ship blasted ours. They were destroying the lifeboats. Fuel leaked into space.

My fellow volunteers knew that it was a lost cause. They evacuated the ship, taking the remaining lifeboats.

I didn't want to leave.

They left. I stayed.

The Prometheans eventually stopped blasting the ship and started going after the lifeboats. The ship was useless. Most of the fuel had leaked out, and it had become a wandering waste.

But there was hope.

That's why I stayed.

But even though I have many more years left, I would come to my passing long before we reached the next habitable planet. Therefore, I must cocoon myself in one of our hyperbolic chambers. My hope is that you figure a way out before we pass Kerl. The air there can sustain both you and me.

I'm telling you all this because I need you. I need you to wake me up.

16

Dalton shielded his eyes as he stepped outside the tunnel. He jumped down. A metal sound hit his ears. The ground was hard, not what he expected. He brought his foot down again, and metal clanged.

The others had joined him.

His eyes were still adjusting to the bright light. *The Sun*, he thought.

No . . .

He blinked. *It couldn't be.*

Rows and rows of large domes came into focus. They went beyond what the eye could see. Below each dome were miles of dirt. It looked as if each was pulled from the earth.

Dalton frantically looked around.

Metal lined the floors, the walls, and the ceiling leading up to a giant glowing light that lit up the entire room. But it wasn't the Sun. It was a giant fluorescent bulb.

Dalton stumbled. His head was in his hands.

Myha's hands were around his arm, helping to steady him.

"What on Earth?" Jareth asked.

But they weren't on Earth, they couldn't be. The Sun wasn't a fluorescent bulb in a steel sky.

"What is this place?" asked Chad.

Shrink just shook his head in awe.

"Look at that," said Chad, pointing to a window.

Dalton ambled over to the large window that went from the floor to the ceiling. He put his hand against the glass. There was nothing but darkness with pinpoints of light. It was all his eyes could see.

*   *   *

"Can we take off our masks?" Shrink asked.

No one answered right away. Soon the air tanks would run out anyway. They couldn't rely on Dalton's ability to breathe. He had breathed in an impossible amount of pollution, and he was still standing.

"I'll be the guinea pig," said Jareth. "I'm living on borrowed time anyway." He disconnected his air tank and removed the mask. He took a deep breath. "No worries."

Myha, Chad and Shrink removed their masks and discarded their air tanks on the ground.

"I thought we were the only one," said Shrink. "The only city. The last trace of humanity. Look at this. How many are there? Ten, twenty, a hundred? Why didn't *they* leave?"

"Maybe their sensors malfunctioned." Myha took off her jacket and tied it around her waist.

"All of them?" Jareth looked from Myha to Dalton.

Myha shook her head.

"They were probably afraid," said Dalton. "Besides, we don't know that they're all still in there."

"We need to search this place," said Shrink. "There must be someone here who can tell us what's going on."

Jareth stepped upon the steel stairs leading up to the galley way.

The bright light loomed above them. Dalton felt as if it was mocking him. It had tricked him, and now, it was laughing at him.

The galley way led into a wide hallway. Control panels lined either side with empty seats in front of them. Throughout the hallway were blinking red lights. A buzzing sound got louder as they walked down the hall.

Dalton had his pocket knife ready but doubted it would be any help. *What if they have Phasers? Or something worse?*

They. Dalton couldn't imagine that they were like him. Why wouldn't they have tried to signal to the people of the cities that it was okay to come out? Where had they been taking them?

Dalton led the way down the adjoining hallway. Fluid-filled chambers, large enough to fit someone inside, lined the wall. Dalton spotted a door.

The door opened when Dalton stood in front of it. Inside were lockers.

Myha opened one. She reached inside and pulled out packets.

"Toss me one," said Jareth.

Myha tossed him a packet.

Jareth opened it and smelled the contents. "It smells like sugar." He put his finger inside and licked it.

"We don't know how long that's been there," Dalton warned.

"It tastes alright," said Jareth.

"It might not be food." Chad swiped it from Jareth's hands, and it fell onto the floor.

"Hey, you little shit."

Dalton opened another locker. There were more packets inside. *If this is food, why would they leave it? Maybe they had to leave in a panic? They could have taken us and then abandoned us. We were less important than whatever they were up against.*

Dalton slammed his hand against the locker. *We were too late. If Dr. Anderson hadn't stopped everyone from realizing the truth, we could have escaped the city. Maybe before all this happened. Being in these domes made us all vulnerable, and something took advantage.*

Dalton leaned his back against the lockers. Maybe those sensors were wrong all along. Maybe they malfunctioned like any other machine. That's why the others didn't go off. UTC Z3T's sensors were the ones that malfunctioned.

He put his head in his hands. He could feel Myha's small hand on his arm.

"We'll find a way back into the city," she said.

Dalton put his hand out. "Through concrete walls?"

"We'll get into another city," Shrink suggested.

"Fat chance," said Jareth. "If those cities are as heavily fortified as ours, dynamite won't work. The doors can't open from the outside. That would defeat the purpose."

Dalton's eyes darted from side to side. That could be it too. They did try to warn us by setting off the sensors. Maybe the world really did go to shit and we were evacuated, evacuated inside our impenetrable cities. But something happened, and they had to leave us. They had to survive.

The more Dalton racked his brain, the more theories started floating around his head. *What does it matter?* Dalton thought. We're on some sort of vessel in the middle of nowhere. We went from one prison into a bigger one.

"Dalton, we have to keep looking," said Myha. "I don't know about you, but I didn't do everything I did back in UTC to come out without answers."

Dalton looked up. How could her eyes still be so damn hopeful?

Myha offered him her hand. He took it, and she helped him to his feet.

The sound was still buzzing in the hallway. They stopped to rest along the way. The ship was so *large*. Shrink glanced at his digital watch.

"It's been three hours," he said. "I'm tired. You guys don't understand. I've never been ten feet away from a chair in my life!"

"There must be a better way around here," said Jareth. "A hovercar or something."

"Well, it doesn't look like there's anyone around to tell us," said Dalton. "These halls are empty. I don't see any hovercars, do you? If we stay here, we can't find proper food or water or a way off this thing. We have to keep going."

They walked for another hour. Dalton's feet were like lead, and his stomach tightened. They followed the sound to a large room full of seats bolted to the floor and more control panels. A large window overlooked the dark sky with its millions of tiny suns, all too far away to resemble the light Dalton had seen in his dreams.

Dalton stepped forward onto the platform above the other seats. A light was glowing red on the control panel. It was glowing above a symbol. He didn't understand what it meant.

"Where did they all go?" Myha wondered.

"Maybe they found the exit," said Dalton, still staring at the control panel. He spoke so low, he doubted she could hear him over the blare of the buzzing.

Dalton turned to face them. He wanted to say, *I'm a fool. We all are. Now, we're going to die here.* But looking at their faces, he knew there was no point in saying that. They already knew.

Suddenly, a projection appeared over the controls. "Hello! I am Urtel Tuvesri. If you are understanding this . . ."

Dalton leaned towards the screen.

"I figured you might want to see some of what your world used to be, so I made this slideshow, set to Bob Dylan's "When the Deal Goes Down." A lazy tune played. Images of green pastures, blue skies, and the Sun appeared peering over the horizon. There were creatures that Dalton had never seen before, some large and small. Some standing in the green pastures and another with big, floppy ears, running to a man, and licking his hand.

"When we landed on your planet, many of us were surprised to find that you had walled yourself into domed cities. There were one hundred and four. With the threat of your star engulfing you, we had to evacuate you immediately. I wanted to save you all, but alas, we were not able to get you out of the fortresses. The ship was only large enough to house five domed cities. I got to pick one.

"I volunteered to stay here. That's what I do: save other lifeforms. I'm particularly fond of humans. We have a satellite planet also inhabited by the Kerls. They are friendly little guys. Compatible with humans, I think.

"On the course the ship is going, in about one millennium, we should be within distance to land on the Kerl planet. The ship cannot land on its own, so I will need to guide it onto the planet, which is why I'm going to need you to wake me up. When the lights flash green, we are within range and you should let me out of my hyperbolic chamber. We will be within range of the planet for two-hundred years.

"Once that time passes, the lights flash red. In that case, I'm sorry, we've missed our mark. The chance was slim anyway. When you let me out of the chamber, I will either get to rejoice with you or cry with you. Either way, it will be an academic accomplishment to meet you."

* * *

They stood in front of Urtel Tuvesri's hyperbolic chamber. It was in a hallway lined with other fluid-filled chambers just like it.

"Should we let the guy out?" asked Shrink.

"Seems kinda crazy to me," said Chad. "He might wanna stick probes up our asses."

Urtel's skin was golden brown. He didn't have any hair on his head or body. Dalton thought he saw a tail wrapped around his leg, but his face was like a man's. His eyes were slightly larger, and his head was bigger. His nostrils were also extraordinarily wide.

Dalton recalled the animated face he saw on the screen and had some difficulty imagining he was the same person trapped in a peaceful sleep.

"It would be cruel," said Dalton. "We would be waking him up into a world that has no hope."

"He might know of somewhere else we could go." Myha touched the glass.

"He would have mentioned it." Dalton turned away from the hyperbolic chamber.

They ate the goopy stuff they found in the lockers. Dalton noticed he needed very little of it to feel full and energized.

"It doesn't taste the best, but it's fine to eat," Urtel had said. "It kept me alive for hundreds of years."

Urtel had mentioned he wanted to try pizza and doughnuts. Dalton found himself wishing he had brought him some.

Dalton sat with Myha. They gazed out of the large window into the abyss of darkness and light.

Dalton remembered a story he had read set on the ocean. About a man so obsessed, he destroyed himself.

Dalton had escaped a sinking ship only to find that the waters outside were rough, and there was no land for miles. At least on the sinking ship, he had food and water and a false sense of comfort.

"It's over, isn't it?" Dalton asked. He didn't want to believe it. It felt like a dream, and only her confirmation could make it true.

Myha leaned her head against his shoulder. "I guess it is."

His world was suddenly a tremendous ocean. He was small. He was afraid.

* * *

Dalton stood in front of the chamber that held the sleeping Urtel Tuvesri. Urtel's face was expressionless. He had no idea that they had been too late.

Urtel has lived hundreds of years, thought Dalton. I was starting to think if something greater cared about me, I would feel special, important, but looking at how vast it is out there . . . out there in space, I don't know if I'll ever feel important again.

Dalton looked at the open chamber beside Urtel's.

Maybe I'll dream of Earth as it was before all this happened. Maybe I'll be with Myha there instead of here on this abandoned vessel.

He stepped into the chamber. The glass doors closed, and fluid began to fill the small compartment.

Dalton held his breath.

excerpt

If you enjoyed UNITED TRACE, look out for

THE WINGS OF HEAVEN AND HELL

Book One of the Arcadian Steel Sequence

By L. M. Peralta

one

HE arch of his wings rose above his head. The tips stretched out to the corners of the sky. His soft, blond hair contrasted against the hardened features of his face. He cast his golden eyes down to his staff, deep in the belly of a beast with many eyes and teeth like the pointed studs on a black, leather jacket. Flames erupted around the two figures still in the canvas and yet alive.

The acrid, bitter taste of turpentine and the smell of linseed oil permeated the room. Heat came off the standing work light which forced the shadows into the corners. Deflated paint tubes littered the floor. Stacks of unused canvases leaned against each other on the wall. *For Whom the Bell Tolls* played over the old stereo covered in paint.

A ladder was propped up alongside the finished painting. The top of the ladder reached the tips of the angel's wings. The angel's eyes unnerved me. They seemed to twitch and vibrate like fire in the breeze. The image seemed so…real.

"You like it?" Dad swished a paintbrush in the water of a gallon jug with the top cut off.

His shoulder length, ruddy brown hair was tied back in a ponytail, but a few strands escaped, matted to the sheen of sweat on his brow. He wore a golden cross, wrapped in silver thorns, around his neck.

I nodded. "Who's it going to?"

"A little gallery on Bienville."

I raised an eyebrow. "A *little* gallery?"

"Diavolo." He smirked.

"Marcus Diavolo! Dad, why didn't you say something?"

"I gave his secretary my portfolio last week. I wanted to know for sure first before I said anything to you and your mom. Didn't want to disappoint you."

"You wouldn't have disappointed me. I don't care what the world thinks."

He smiled at me while he dried the paintbrush with a worn rag.

"You need to tell Mom," I said. "She's going to *die* when she finds out."

"No, no, no," he said. "We have something much more important to celebrate tonight. It's your sweet sixteen. You won't get away that easily."

I groaned. "I'm a little too old for birthday parties." I *was* sixteen. At least, that's how old I supposed I was.

No one knew my birthday. I know weird, right? I didn't have a birth certificate. So, my parents made November 11ᵗʰ my honorary birthday. The 11th of November, ten years ago, was the day they adopted me, the day my whole life changed for the better.

Micah and Alexandria Hebert were the only parents I'd ever known. I was found alone in an abandoned house when I was too small for kindergarten. The house was on the market for ages, and the owners lived in Tennessee. They had no idea who I was.

"Li, you know how your mom feels about this. You're the only little girl she'll ever have." He put his arm around my shoulder. "You can celebrate teenage-style with your friends this weekend."

My friends. Yeah, if I had any. I used to have a lot of friends before high school. Felicia Drake and I were friends since first grade. That was until she made it her personal mission to make my life hell. I didn't ask for Mike Breyers to look at me. I wasn't interested in him. He was on the football team, and Felicia had a known crush on him which made him off limits to anyone else. When he asked me to the Spring Dance, she all but lost it.

All throughout freshman year, I would find gum stuck to my locker and get tripped in the hallway by Felicia or one of her new friends. Felicia spread rumors about me and made passive aggressive comments every chance she got. By my sophomore year, the whole school thought I was adopted because my bio-mom went to jail for prostitution, and my birth father was her pimp. So, no, I didn't have any friends. Unless I could count my dad.

"Come on, what do you say?" He squeezed my shoulder.

I laughed. "Dad, you'll get paint on me." I shrugged away from him. "Alright, we can celebrate, but I'll secretly be celebrating this." I motioned to the painting. "Diavolo. Wow."

"Thanks, sweetie." He looked at the backs of his hands and at his palms, covered in paint. Several more splotches stained his white t-shirt. "Can you get the radio? I'm going to jump in the shower." He worked all night. Dad said the muses came for him in the dark. "After school, when your mom gets home, we'll have cake, presents, and we'll drive into the city for dinner."

"Okay." I lifted my backpack from the concrete floor. "I don't want to go anyplace fancy."

Dad winked. "I would never do that to you."

I rolled my eyes and smirked.

"I gotta go." I shouldered my backpack.

"Don't let school ruin your education," he said. He echoed the words of Mark Twain. Although, I'm not sure Dad knew Twain said that first.

I laughed. "I would never do that to you." If not for the history exam in fourth period, I would have skipped school. I bet Dad wouldn't mind if I stayed in my room all day on my guitar. But I didn't do so well in history. I crinkled my nose.

I left the music of Dad's studio behind. I arrived at the corner right as the bus pulled up. The doors screeched open, cutting through the silence of the morning. I took a seat in the back and put my headphones on. *Fear of the Dark* blared in my ears as the bus took off.

The houses blurred through the windows until the bus entered the city and stopped at a light. A man stood at the corner. He wore baggy clothes and a faded baseball cap. Something twitched at the base of his jacket. I turned my attention to the upholstery of the seat in front of me. I didn't want to look back and see its eyes. The eyes were always what got me.

The bus stopped outside St. Andrews, and I walked to class. In third period, I stared at my history test like it was written in Latin. My pen was in my mouth more than it scribbled along the page. The lunch bell rang before I could answer the last question.

At lunch, I sat alone. Friendships were difficult to maintain with a malicious sixteen-year-old spreading lies about me.

"Nice t-shirt," said Felicia. She stood at my table with her gaggle of giggling girls who dressed like her and acted like her. They wore monochromatic colors and heels that I might die in. Felicia's hand reached the side of her lunch tray. Before I could react, her hand with long, polished onyx black nails gripped the plastic fork and catapulted a forkful of coleslaw at me. The coleslaw plummeted onto my t-shirt and covered my left shoulder in mayo, cabbage, and vinegar hell.

"Oops." She covered her mouth with her hand.

Heat rose at my temples. Felicia was the only one in school who knew today was my birthday. I didn't get into fights, and I wouldn't let Felicia Drake ruin my birthday with a trip to the principal's office.

Felicia's heels clicked along the laminate cafeteria room floor. She laughed with the other girls. Her heels were at least three inches high, not that she needed the extra height.

Fall, fall, fall.

She didn't.

I grabbed a handful of napkins and scooped up the mess from my shoulder. The vinegar stung my nose. I tossed the napkins in my tray and threw the rest of my lunch in the garbage. The food didn't taste that good anyway. Soon, I would get ice cream and cake courtesy of my mom.

I went to the bathroom to get the rest of the coleslaw off my shirt, hoping to get the smell out. Armed with a handful of paper towels from the dispenser, I wet them in the sink and leaned in to peer into the mirror and see where the stain was. A sizable white smear was on my black t-shirt and bits of cabbage hung from my shoulder. I wiped at the stain with the towels. I made progress, but the smell lingered.

One fluorescent light blinked on and off. Coldness crept onto my skin. My sweater's arms were tied securely around my waist. I should have put the sweater on before the cold turned my fingernails purplish-blue.

A dark form blurred at the edge of my vision. I tried not to look. I didn't see them more than two or three times a week, and when I did, I tried to ignore them. But this time I couldn't ignore the dark shape reflected in the mirror. The thing crouched in the corner of the bathroom. The creature was thin with skin the color of charcoal and a bald, bulbous head. It faced away from me toward the wall. It shook and whimpered.

Before my parents adopted me, family services took me to a string of psychologists. I saw them. Horrible monsters. They said my hallucinations were a result of what I went through, being abandoned by my bio-mom. That they weren't there.

"Not there. Not there. Not there," I chanted and closed my eyes.

Thud! Tap. Tap. My fingertips squeezed the ceramic surface of the sink. *Did it move?* But I didn't dare open my eyes. I continued to chant.

"What are you doing?" Felicia's voice bounced off the walls.

My eyes shot open.

"*Not there. Not there*," she mocked. "No matter how many times you wish that wasn't the face staring back at you, your reflection will always be the same. So, you can give up."

I glared at her. "You got coleslaw all over my shirt. I smell like vinegar and mayonnaise. Today's my birthday. I know you know that. Did you have to come in here and—"

I broke off. Crimson eyes, wide and round like headlights stained red after a hit-and-run, stared at me through the glass.

My breath trapped in my lungs. I turned away from the mirror.

"You can cry if you want to," said Felicia.

I pushed past her and into the hallway.

The rest of the day, I wore my sweater in class to smother the smell of vinegar. I couldn't get the stain out, and even the thick cotton of my sweater didn't work hard enough to mask the smell. I hoped only I could smell the harsh aroma since the fumes were on me.

I should have taken off my shirt in the bathroom and just worn my sweater, but I wasn't going into another school bathroom, not for a long time. My skin prickled. Was the creature still huddled in the corner? What did it want?

The bell rang. I folded my pen into my notebook and pinned the notebook to my chest. The teacher fought to finish her sentence over the flutter of paper, chatter, and the shuffle of feet. I picked up my backpack and slung one strap onto my shoulder as I headed out the classroom. With my head down, I marched down the hallway. The sun hit my face as I made for the entrance of the school and I ducked my head lower. My hair veiled the sides of my face. I collided into someone. Michael Breyers.

His gray-blue eyes anchored me. "Lia."

I turned to look over my shoulder. Felicia and her troop passed through the doors of the school. She would hate it if she saw me talking to Mike. So, that's what I did. She was over him, but a little light conversation would remind her of my betrayal.

"Hi, Mike," I said. I didn't flirt. I talked about the history mid-term, but I knew that was enough.

Felicia glared at me as she passed.

Mike was on the football team so he turned the conversation to the big game. I ignored him as he droned on.

A man stood across the street from the school. His eyes were on me. His hair was black, but his skin was pale as if never touched by sunlight. I knew that was wrong though. He had been touched by something brighter than the sun. He wore a white t-shirt with a leather jacket and jeans. On his hands were black gloves. Something white arched above his shoulders on either side.

"Lia, did you hear me?"

My eyes were again tethered to Mike's. "Yeah. I have to go." I ripped my gaze away.

I walked home. In a little less than an hour, I was inside. I dropped my backpack at the door. Mom would be home from work any minute.

The bracelets on my wrists knocked against each other as I gripped the bannister and jogged up the stairs.

I opened the door to my bedroom. Posters made the walls invisible. AC/DC, Led Zeppelin, Black Sabbath, and R.E.M. held up the ceiling. The floor was a bed of unwashed clothes. My Firebird leaned against the wall next to the amp. One of the strings popped the last time I played. Beside my desk was a waste basket full of the crumpled remains of several failed drafts of an essay I worked on for class.

The essay was on Colonialism in early America. The essay wasn't my greatest venture. Studying history was as dull as listening to music through earmuffs. The paper was due next Friday. I sighed.

Sim wandered into my room. She stretched her long feline body and sauntered over to me. I reached down to stroke her fur. "There you are, girl," I said. She meowed.

Sim disappeared in the house. She went missing for hours. Dad thought the house harbored a crawlspace we didn't know about and that Sim wandered into the hole from time to time. The house was old. Dad inherited the home from his mother. I never met her. Both my parents' parents died before they adopted me.

I took off my Kiss shirt. It still held the faint scent of vinegar. I picked up a black t-shirt from the floor and pressed my nose into the fabric. I shrugged, pulled the shirt on over my tank top, and took a quick glance in the standing mirror in the corner of my room. My fingers combed through my long hair, light brown and dyed reddish-pink at the ends. My blood red nail polish looked like tiny misshaped hearts in the center of each fingernail. My nose ring looped over the edge of one nostril.

I flashed a smile and headed out the bedroom door. The front door squealed open as I took the stairs two at a time.

Mom walked in, juggling her purse and a white cake box. She wore flats because heels made her *too* tall. Slim with hair the color of charcoal that flowed down her back like ink, she wore a patterned dress and a dark blazer.

People who didn't know I was adopted said I looked like my dad. Maybe that was because I was so different from my mom. She was a tall, raven beauty, while I was short, right under five two with light brown hair and almond shaped eyes. Mom's skin was light as cream, and mine was tannish and darkened easily in the sun.

"Hey, Mom, can I help you with that?" I grabbed the box from her.

"Thanks, honey. Can you put that on the counter for me?" she asked.

"Sure thing."

She walked down the hall and turned. "Oh, and Happy Birthday!"

"You told me twice this morning, Ma."

She smiled. "I know, baby, and I'll probably say it twice more before the day is out."

I smiled back, shook my head, and rolled my eyes. I set the cake on the counter. A knock sounded at the front door.

Uncle Jonah stood on the porch. His eyes were bloodshot. "Happy Birthday, Li!" He grinned and kissed me on the forehead.

"Hey," I said. "Cake's on the table. Just waiting on Mom and Dad."

Jonah wrung his hands as he walked in. His eyes darted as if afraid someone might jump him.

"You okay?" I asked.

"Sure, sure. I gotta use the bathroom." He wandered down the hall and into the guest bathroom.

Meanwhile, Dad came down the stairs. He wore jeans and a t-shirt. His hair was loose and stringy around his face.

"Did you get a chance to tell Mom the good news?" I asked.

He put his arm around my shoulders and led me into the kitchen. "Shh," he said. "I'll tell her tomorrow. Today's about you, kid."

I wished for a button I could press to set my eyes on roll.

Mom walked into the kitchen. "Okay," she said, "let's cut the cake." Her words came out in a rush of air as if she had been holding her breath.

"Wait," I said. "Uncle Jonah's here. He's in the bathroom."

A look of concern crossed Mom's face. Dad narrowed his eyes as Jonah made his way into the kitchen. He stumbled as he approached the counter. Jonah put his arms around Dad. At first, Dad's arms hung limp, but slowly he brought one up to pat Jonah on the back.

Mom smiled, tight-lipped, and opened the box. She removed the cake which she placed on the table. She took out a box of matches from a drawer in the kitchen and lit the three candles. On the cake, written in curly frosting cursive, were the words: *Happy Birthday, Lia!* They came at me like a neon sign as if I hadn't heard those words enough. I waited through the cringe-y Happy Birthday song and blew out the candles.

Mom beamed, and tears squeezed from the corners of her eyes. I wrapped my arms around her waist and gave her a quick hug. "Thanks, Mom."

She cut the cake, and we all sat on the sofa in the living room while we ate. The sofa faced a brick fireplace. The television was mounted above the mantel. Dad's paintings hung on the walls. A girl stood in a white gown with a raven perched on her head. A dark snake floated through the mazelike cluster of leafless trees rising from the mist. A man sat bent over a heavy book, his face blurred out like a drop of blood in the water.

The airiness of the cake settled on my tongue. Crumbs found their way into my lap. The sharp sweetness of frosting awakened my taste buds as I licked my lips.

Dad finished first and set his plate on the coffee table. He got up and moved behind the sofa. When he came back, he held a box wrapped in silver paper. The box was roughly four feet long and half as wide.

"What's this?" I asked as he placed the box in front of me on the coffee table. Sim weaved between my ankles.

"Open it," he said.

I knelt by the table and ripped off the wrapping paper. I took the top off the box. A black guitar case nestled inside. I flipped open the latch. In the case, a guitar lay in a bed of velvet, but not just any guitar. The instrument was a Fender Stratocaster with a lacquer black finish and maple neck, the same guitar played by Pink Floyd guitarist David Gilmour. I cradled the guitar in my hands.

My eyes widened. I looked up at Dad. "This must have cost you a fortune."

"We've been saving up for it since you were nine years old."

I placed the guitar against my chest and strummed a few notes. The notes carried through the air like whispers. The guitar needed an amp. A Frontman sat in my room for my old Firebird. I couldn't wait to hook up the Strat and play it.

"Hey, I got you something too." Uncle Jonah shoved a small box into my line of vision.

I knit my brows and stowed the guitar back in its case. I opened the box Uncle Jonah handed me. A small heart-shaped locket slid inside the box. It looked antique, not my style, but I was so excited about my new guitar I didn't care. "Thanks," I said.

"Why don't you try it on?" he encouraged.

I smiled thin-lipped. "Okay." I clasped the chain around my neck. The heart-shaped locket dangled upon my black Metallica t-shirt.

"Looks good on you," said Jonah.

"Yeah, I guess," I said. I wanted to get back to my Strat.

Uncle Jonah grumbled something about needing to use the bathroom. He stood and ambled out of the room.

Dad sat down next to me, and I hugged him and Mom. "Thank you so much. A Strat. I can't wait to play it on my Frontman."

"Where do you want to go eat, kiddo?" Dad asked.

"I don't know." I shrugged. "Wherever you guys want to go. I'm good with anything." My eyes swept over the guitar. "I'll be good with anything for a long time."

"How about Urban Ambience?" Dad asked.

"That's all the way in the city," Mom said.

"Yeah, but how often do we get to go out there. It's still early. Plus, you can get that drink you like."

"Well," she said, "we better leave now." She got up from the sofa. I'll go grab my purse. Micah, you might want to check on Jonah. He's been in there an awful long time."

Mom disappeared into the hallway, and Dad walked over to the guest bathroom. He banged on the door. "Jonah, everything okay in there?"

I approached the hallway and listened from the other side of the wall.

"Just a minute," Jonah yelled. The door creaked open, and a thud shook the wall.

"You're high, aren't you?" Dad's voice was tense.

"No," Jonah stammered.

"How dare you, Jonah? You came to my little girl's birthday party high, and you're doing drugs in my bathroom?"

"I wasn't…"

"Oh, yeah. Then, what's that?"

Jonah murmured something I couldn't hear.

"Get it out of here," Dad said.

Feet marched down the hallway, and the front door slammed. I walked into the hall. Dad's arm leaned against the doorframe. His head was down.

"You made him leave?" I asked.

Dad rubbed his eyes.

I shook my head. "He can't help it, Dad. You said to treat people the way you want to be treated, but you've never treated Uncle Jonah that way. You always kick him out."

Mom reached the bottom of the stairs. She put her hands on my shoulders. "Uncle Jonah has a problem," she said.

"But he can't help it."

"It's the kind of problem that's not safe for him or us."

"Uncle Jonah would never do anything to hurt us."

"Not on purpose," Mom said. "We can talk about it when we get home. I don't want you to miss dinner. It's still a school night. How about a rain check? Deal?"

I was quiet for a moment. Uncle Jonah was sick. Dad knew it. I wished he didn't kick him to the curb like that. You don't do that to family. But the hopeful and concerned look in Mom's eyes told me this was not the time to discuss Uncle Jonah's problem. I didn't want to ruin this day for her.

I nodded. "Deal."

STREET lamps spotlighted the interstate. Darkness shrouded the lake. The headlights of passing cars cast odd shadows inside Dad's sedan. I nodded to *Eulogy* as the song blared over the radio, and the rain battered against the windows.

Mom leaned over and put a hand on Dad's arm. She smiled at him. The smile said *I'm happy* and *I love you* without the words. Mom was always good at saying what she meant with an expression or a touch. Dad smiled back.

I wanted to tell Mom that Dad got into the Diavolo gallery. She'd be ecstatic, but I couldn't do that to him. He wanted to wait to tell her. Maybe he'd tell her tonight after dinner. I imagined the look on her face: a smile erupted, and her eyes crinkled to the point of tearing up.

Dad's work belonged in the Diavolo gallery. His paintings were as dark and passionate as rock and roll. I shivered. The angel's eyes punctured my consciousness. He was canvas, nothing more. Art should give you goose bumps sometimes, right?

The rain melted down the window as the railing of the bridge raced. I wanted to bang out a few songs on the guitar. I couldn't play all night. Mom needed to go to work in the morning.

After two or three songs, I'd head down to the living room to watch TV and eat ice cream till two in the morning. I would be groggy when the bus came the next morning, but I'd settle for tiredness if it meant staying up watching bad movies and playing my Strat.

Lightning ripped the sky and jolted my focus to the front windshield.

Mom screamed.

Something slammed onto the front of the car. The back tires left the ground, and the hood crushed under the pressure.

Wings spread against the sky. White feathers loosed in the wind. A staff impaled into the body of the car. The angel's eyes fixed on me. The eyes moved like they reflected flames.

The angel kicked off the car, and I felt weightless.

We tumbled. Metal skid against the road. The sedan headed for the concrete guardrail. I screamed as the radio continued to blare on.

Glass around me shattered, but didn't touch me. The car groaned as pressure caused the front of the vehicle to flatten like a soda can. The seat beside me was caved in, but I was safe. My side hurt from the impact, and I was shaken but otherwise unharmed. The car was turned upside down. The rain stopped.

I unbuckled my seatbelt and fell to the roof of the car. Blood dripped, and my vision blurred.

"Mom, Dad?"

Their bodies dangled from their seats. I reached for Mom's seatbelt.

"Don't, honey," she said. "My legs. They're stuck."

The dashboard crushed her legs, and blood slid over her jeans. The car's windshield was cracked all over.

"I can get you out." I tried to sound hopeful for me and for her.

Dad's hand was on mine. His head lulled back and forth. Heat fought against the misty cold.

Dad let go of my hand. A mixture of pain and sadness lit upon his face. "Go, go. Run!" The words sounded difficult for him to get out as if his lungs were collapsed.

"I can't leave you." My eyes reflected the flames.

His jaw clenched. His face rang with urgency, fear, and something else: regret. The regret wasn't because he was dying, although he didn't want to, regret because he wanted to say goodbye the right way. He cared about stuff like that. But he couldn't say goodbye the right way because he would feel guilty if he didn't use his last words to save me. That was all he cared about, but I cared too, and I wouldn't let them die.

"Mom?"

She looked at me. Blood trailed down her forehead. Her hand stroked the side of my face, and she smiled that smile that said *I love you*.

The wind ripped through me as an invisible force threw me from the car. I rolled along the road until I stopped belly down palms against the ground. I rose on my knees. My feet were unsteady. I tried to run back to the car. "No!" I screamed, my hand outstretched.

The car went up in an explosion of flames and knocked me to the ground. My body melted into the asphalt. Tears ran down my face. My whole world changed.

Sobs racked me so hard I felt like someone punched me in the chest. I held my hands against the ache. A shadow, faint in the dim, veiled me in deeper darkness.

A man stood over me, a man with wings like the creature who landed on our car. I shuddered. But something put me at ease unlike the terror as I gazed into the eyes of the one like him. His eyes were melted gold, and they shone like metal.

The mist curled around us.

"Who are you?" My voice cracked.

"You *can* see me." He squinted like I was something impossible when he was the one with wings.

"Of course," I said. "But why are you dressed like that?"

He wore a long-sleeved shirt with gloves to cover his hands. The material was metallic like silver. Several cuts marred the fabric. *And was that a sword at his side?*

Like a knight out of the Middle Ages, he had a sword with a silver hilt that hung in a sheath at his side. *Had this man, if I could call him that, fought that monster who attacked us?*

Flames still flared from the sedan. I clung to him. "My parents, you have to help my parents." The chances were slim, but I saw other impossible things that night. "Please," I begged.

The golden-eyed stranger shook his head. "They're gone, and you have to come with me."

I rubbed my temples. I must have hit my head when I was thrown from the car. Maybe I was hallucinating. I might have gotten a concussion when I hit the ground. *No, you were seeing things before you were thrown from the car.* I wasn't hallucinating, I just wished I was. This winged stranger asked me to go with him. "I can't. I don't even know you."

"I'm Adriel. I can protect you. But coming with me isn't really up to you."

I gaped at him. "You want to kidnap me?" I reached into my back pocket for my phone. He didn't try to stop me. Dizzy, I backed away and pressed the speed dial for Jonah.

"Uncle Jonah?"

"Lia? How's everything going, hon?" His words were slow.

"We were attacked," I said.

"Attacked? Where are you?" Jonah's voice was clarity mixed with panic.

"We got into an accident on the bridge." My thoughts were clearer. I didn't want to look at the winged man who stood a couple feet from me. I didn't want to admit what I was seeing. *Not now. No time for crazy now.* "Please, come. I think Mom and Dad are dead." I sobbed out the last words. I didn't know if he heard.

"Oh, my God, Li. Stay right where you are. I'm calling the police."

The call ended, and the screen faded to black.

"We don't have time to wait for the police," said Adriel, "and they won't be able to keep you safe."

Keep me safe? My parents were gone. No one would keep me safe anymore. *The world is a lyre, and its music is sorrow.*

My head swam. I fell, but Adriel caught me before I hit the ground, right before everything went dark.

Two

IS eyes were cobalt blue, not the eyes of evil, but I grinned in relish while he burned. His staff lie useless on the ground as my fingers curled around his neck. And all around us angels fell. They plunged from the sky, fiery like shooting stars.

My eyelids were difficult to open like honey crusted over them. I blinked. The bed was soft beneath me. Above me was an off-white ceiling and a dusty fan. Dull orange light poured in.

I hauled myself onto my elbows. Every muscle in my body ached, and my skin felt bruised all over. A television sat in the hollowed-out wardrobe.

A presence lingered near me. I glanced to my left. A pair of wings consumed my vision. He stood by the window with his back to me. I yelped and scrambled to the other side of the bed.

"You're awake." Adriel turned, and I breathed a sigh. I didn't understand why his presence brought me such relief, but it did.

A headache was coming on. I rubbed my temples. "Where am I?"

"You're at a motel," said Adriel. "I fought him off. But I was afraid he might return."

"Who?"

"The one who attacked you."

Adriel wore a dark jacket over a white t-shirt and black jeans. A dozen horizontal cuts patterned the jeans, like he got into a knife fight. No, the rips were the style of the jeans unless the knife fight was with a dwarf or someone who crouched a lot.

I hoped that the stranger who pulled me from the scene of a car crash and watched me from my school wasn't the type of guy who got into knife fights.

Although the silvery armor he wore the night before also bore a pattern of cuts. That night, he had a sword. *Where was that weapon now? Had I imagined it? Was I imagining him?*

His wings glimmered in and out of focus like my mind was trying to reject their existence.

I approached him.

"Stand back," he said. "And don't touch me."

I narrowed my eyes. If anyone should be scared, that person was me. Whoever this man was, he had wings like the monster who killed my parents. But despite that, this odd sense of comfort lingered around him, more than comfort. I felt as if he could protect me from anything.

"What the hell is going on?" I asked.

The room smelled musty. The comforter lay at the foot of the bed. I must have kicked the blanket off me last night. Did he watch me sleep?

My danger meter should have been off the charts, but for some odd reason this perfect stranger made me feel safe. He was so familiar.

He stared out the door's peephole. He moved to the window and pulled back the curtain enough for him to peer outside.

I was transfixed by the white wings on his back. A glow came off them, like the moon against the dark sky.

"Hello?"

"You'll be safe here at least till morning." He didn't look at me, but continued to peer out the window.

"Safe? What are you talking about? Why would I *not* be safe?"

"Do I have to remind you what happened out there?" He turned around and faced me.

He was tall, more than a head taller than me anyway. His eyes were bright like a light shined behind them. He pushed all the darkness away.

I forced my eyes shut and shook my head. No, he didn't have to remind me that my parents were dead, that a beautiful monster hurdled onto their car and pierced me with those horrible eyes.

Adriel turned away to look out the window one last time before he closed the curtains to the morning light.

"What are you doing?" I asked. "I won't stay here with a stranger in a Halloween costume." I grabbed the door handle. Before I could turn the knob, his gloved hand was around my wrist.

"If you go, he will find you." His voice was a whisper but held more power than any words I'd ever heard spoken.

My heart dropped. Could he mean the man who murdered Mom and Dad? But that was in my head.

"*He* who?" I asked.

"Raphael."

"The painter?"

"The Archangel."

Did he say *Archangel?*

"Um." I didn't know what to say. They couldn't be real. A licensed therapist told me that much. I was in a seedy motel room with a crazy person. Sure, the costume was convincing, but whoever this guy was, he was one of the men who followed me. Maybe he thought I figured out that he belonged to a super-secret gang, and they needed to kill me. But that didn't make any sense either.

I was hospitalized because I told my caseworker that I saw winged people and dark monsters. No one else ever saw them. I was the crazy one. The stress was too much. I was hallucinating again. But I never *talked* to one before. Maybe I should have let them lock me up in a psych ward.

"Look," I said. "I know what I'm seeing isn't real. I mean you have wings, and you're telling me that an Archangel is after me. Oh, my god, what am I saying? This isn't real. I'm talking to a hallucination." I turned my back to him.

My fingers twitched, and I pinched my arm, but I still stood in the motel room, and my parents were still dead.

"You can see us, Lia. No one else can, not if we don't want them to."

How did he know my name?

"This is crazy." I shook my head. *What will I say when the police question me about what happened to my parents?* Maybe they'd give me a psych evaluation and put me on meds. Maybe that's what I needed.

"I guess you forgot Sydriel then," Adriel said.

Sydriel? Why did that name sound so familiar?

"How she disappeared when you were four years old?"

"I don't remember anything." I couldn't remember why I was in foster care in the first place. From what I understand, what I've been told, I was found in an empty house when I was four. My mother and father were gone.

"Sydriel tried to keep you safe, but she disappeared. I thought Raphael got to her. He's looked for you ever since, and he'll keep looking for you."

Could this be real? What should I do? Play along, a voice whispered to me.

"What does Raphael want with me?" I asked. "What could *I* do to an Archangel?"

"You can make them fall." Adriel looked at the floor. His voice was like a ripple in a vast sea, afraid that it might lose itself in greater waters.

"Fall?"

"From grace."

My eyes darted back and forth. I wasn't religious. I went to church a handful of times with Felicia and her parents. I never read the Bible, but I knew enough to convince someone I didn't grow up under a rock.

"I thought only angels that broke away from God could fall," I said.

"That used to be the case until you came along," said Adriel. "Raphael wants to track you down, and I'm going to stop him."

I didn't understand. If an Archangel wanted me dead because I could make angels fall, why was this angel *helping* me? Angels were the good guys, right? I knew enough about religion to know that.

Alien life might exist, but who is to say that aliens will be anything like what we think. What if that is the same for angels? *Were* they the good guys?

Adriel's eyes fastened me in place. I didn't see anything in his eyes that might indicate that he had lied to me, but something else made me want to coil myself into a tight, safe ball. The liquid gold turned hard.

To protect someone that you hated would be challenging. Still, if he hated me, he wouldn't have protected me in the first place.

"But, what are you going to do?" I asked.

Adriel shook his head. "I don't know. But that's not what's important right now. I have to make sure that Raphael doesn't find you, or we all will suffer the consequences."

"Well, that's a bit horrifying."

"I've kept you safe here for a few days, but tomorrow, we have to leave."

"Wait. How long have I been here?" I asked.

"Two days."

Horror flashed through me as if cold water was poured down my shirt. "Two days! I need to call my uncle." I searched my pockets for my phone.

"That's not a good idea," he said.

"Where's my phone?"

Adriel shook his head. "Raphael will find you."

I glanced at him. I tasted salt as I tried to blink the tears away. "The last time I spoke to my uncle, I told him I'd been attacked, and my parents were dead. He's the only family I have left. Now, give me my damn phone."

Adriel withdrew my cellphone from his pocket and tossed it onto the bed. I snatched the phone and called Uncle Jonah.

He picked up before the second ring. "Li?"

"Yeah, it's me."

"Oh, thank God." His voice was warm liquid rubbed into cracked and callous fingers. "Where are you? Are you alright?"

"I'm fine," I said.

"They said you were in an accident, that the car hydroplaned and got crushed against the guardrail," said Jonah. "They found your parents. I'm so sorry, Li."

My breath caught. I hoped this was a nightmare. That my parents were fine and that they waited at home for me.

"At first, the police thought you died when the car went up. I told them I talked to you, but they didn't know if that was before or after the car combusted. I made the arrangements for all three of you. But the coroner called yesterday. Said you weren't in the car with them. The police said you might have walked away. That you might have been confused because of a concussion. They're looking for you."

"Arrangements?" I asked.

"The funeral is today," he said. "There wasn't much left." He sobbed over the phone. I waited and listened to his sobs. He sniffled. "I'm sorry I planned the funeral without you. Until yesterday, I thought you were gone too."

I gripped the phone. "What time?" I asked.

"What?"

"What time are they burying my parents?"

"At ten."

"Okay." I ended the call. The phone slipped from my hand and onto the bed. I felt my heart compress into a hard pebble. My cheeks were sticky with tears.

Adriel sat in the worn chair by the window. His wings swept out on either side of the chair. He leaned forward and watched me.

"You have to let me go." I wanted to be strong, but my voice reminded me of a guitar string breaking. "My parents' funeral is today."

"I can't do that," said Adriel. "Not with Raphael on your trail."

"I'll call the police," I said. "I'll say you kidnapped me."

"That won't work."

"They're my parents," I said. "They can't bury them without me."

Adriel's eyes softened like gold in a furnace. "I'll bring you there, but you have to promise to leave with me."

"I don't even know you," I said.

"All you need to know is that I can protect you."

AFTER I washed my face in the motel sink, I gazed in the dingy mirror. My hair was matted to the sides of my face. My fingertips pressed a pink mark, shaped like a toothless smile, along my jaw. The tenderness prepared me for a bruise.

I met Adriel outside the motel. He leaned against a motorcycle in the parking lot. He handed me a helmet.

"A motorcycle? Can't you just fly?"

"I'm not flying you around the city, Lia." He swung his leg over to the other side of the motorcycle. Before I settled in behind him, Adriel's head jerked around.

"Here." He tossed me a pair of black gloves. "Hold onto the grab rail. Don't lean against my wings."

"Isn't that dangerous?" I asked. "Shouldn't I have my hands around your waist?"

"I won't let you fall." He dropped his arm.

The front of the motorcycle was long with handlebars that curved backwards.

I sat behind him and strapped on the helmet. I gripped the metal grab rail that curved from the sides to the back of the motorcycle as Adriel started the engine.

"Hey, what about your helmet?" I asked.

"Believe me," said Adriel. "If I fall, I would be more worried about the ground than my head."

Within minutes, we were outside a café in a squat building with windows lining the front and a few chairs and tables outside.

Adriel got off the motorcycle, and I followed. He reached into his pocket and pulled out a wad of bills, holding it out towards me.

"What's this?"

"Money."

"I know, but it's yours."

"You have money to pay for breakfast?"

"No." The word dragged from my lips.

"Then, take it." He shoved the money into my hand.

"Okay, but I don't need two hundred dollars to buy a cup of coffee and a scone." I took a twenty and handed him back the rest of the bills.

We walked through the glass door. Nestled at the back of the café was a counter where two baristas chatted. A smattering of tables and chairs dotted the room. The odorous smell of coffee brewing assaulted my nostrils.

I never appreciated the pure taste of coffee without any flavoring. For my Mom, the smell was lazy walks through the French Quarter and cold winters in a warm house. For me, the scent of coffee was cramming for a mid-term and a reminder of mornings, which I hated. I didn't drink coffee for the taste, but the ice helped.

The café was empty except for a man with combed hair who sat next to a beautiful woman with long, tussled, blonde locks.

"Do you want anything?" I asked Adriel.

"No," he said.

I approached the counter and ordered an iced coffee and a blueberry scone. The barista with the tight up-do reached into the glass display case with tissue paper and handed me the scone while I waited for my coffee.

I settled down in the chair across from Adriel at a table in the corner of the room. I was stiff and hollow.

I raised the scone to my mouth. "You sure you don't want anything?" I asked guiltily.

"Yes," said Adriel. "I don't eat."

"You don't eat?" I raised an eyebrow.

"I don't need to."

"Okay," I said, "but do you *want* to?"

Adriel was silent. He glanced out the window as if he expected something bad to happen at any moment.

"They can't see you?" I glanced over at the baristas. They gossiped at the counter.

"No," said Adriel. "Only you."

"Lucky me." Blueberry oozed out of the scone and onto my napkin. I wouldn't have been surprised if the jelly found its way to the corner of my lip.

"If only I can see you, how were you able to get that money and the motel room?"

"Others can see me only when I want them to, and *how* I want them to."

Well, that was a great way for a hallucination to explain itself.

"So," I said. "Where are you taking me after…you know?" I wasn't hungry anymore. I flaked off the crust of the scone with my fingernail.

Adriel didn't look at me. He still watched the windows. "Away from here," he said.

"But won't he find me again?" I asked.

"Then we'll move again."

"You want me to go on the run? You do know I'm only sixteen, right? I haven't even finished high school."

"There will be time for that later."

"You mean, when Raphael *stops* hunting me?"

Adriel's eyes fixed on mine. "He won't stop hunting you."

"That was my point," I whispered.

The woman at the other table glanced over at me, a puzzled look on her face.

"Stop talking to me," said Adriel. "People will think you're crazy."

Am I though? I wondered.

THE clouds hung low in the sky. Morning dew dampened the grass. Headstones rose from the ground with names of people who weren't here anymore. I knew only two. I looked at my hands, clasped, as the priest read a passage from the Bible.

Mom's parents died when she was eight, and she aged out of the system. She had no family except Dad, me, and Uncle Jonah. That was part of the reason she was the way she was with me. She wanted me to have what she never did: parents who loved her.

Dad's parents died when he was in his twenties. Mom and Dad had friends, but Uncle Jonah didn't tell them about the ceremony, or else they would have come.

The priest turned to me. "Would you like to say anything?"

I shook my head. My nose stung as the tears started. I took a deep breath. "Why do you believe in God?"

The priest clenched his Bible to his chest. "Because God has provided me a life and a soul and a place to go when I die. He has given you the same opportunity."

Opportunity. I never thought of death as an opportunity. Death was an ending.

The priest placed a hand on my shoulder. He smiled, not showing any teeth. His brows turned down above his eyes.

Jonah stumbled into the ceremony as they lowered the caskets into the ground. He wore a crumpled black suit. His eyes fell to Dad's tombstone which read *Beloved Father, Brother, and Husband. Rocking with the Big Man Upstairs.* His finger and thumb pressed against his eyes as if he could hold the tears in.

Adriel watched me from the tree line. I gulped. I wasn't going with him. He was a stranger. He wanted me to run, but I couldn't do that.

I approached Uncle Jonah. He wiped his tears on the sleeve of his jacket. His hands twitched.

"What's going to happen now?" I asked.

He looked down at his feet. "I have to take you to the caseworker who called me yesterday."

My hands curled into fists, and the muscles in my face tensed.

He reached out to hug me, but I backed away.

"Why?" I asked. "Why can't you take me?"

Uncle Jonah choked back a sob. "I want to, Li, but I can't. The State won't let me. I can't get clean."

My heart felt like it was being squeezed between two brick walls. I raised my fists and hit him in the chest.

He grabbed my arms. "It's okay."

"No, it's not okay," I shouted. "It'll never be okay."

I lost my parents, and I saw something impossible, something that killed them while it stared daggers at me, something that wanted me dead too.

Three

ONAH let go of my wrists, and I slumped against his chest. He hugged me while I cried.

"You have to take me back home." I put space between us and wiped the tears from my eyes.

"I told you. I can't do that," he said.

"Yes, you can. Just for a little while. I want to pick up a few things without some caseworker breathing down my neck."

"Okay." Jonah nodded. "I'll take you, but you have to promise me that you'll go with them. I'll do everything in my power to get you back. I swear to you."

I didn't believe him. Jonah could never give up the drugs. That was what frustrated my parents.

I met Adriel's eyes. They were metal.

"Come on." Uncle Jonah put an arm around my shoulders and led me to the car.

I got into the passenger's seat of his old Pontiac, and he closed the door behind me. White lines ran through the leather upholstery, and the floor of the car was dotted with dry leaves, candy wrappers, and the odd bottle cap. Powdery, white stains mixed with brown and black ones. Particles of dirt settled in the corners and in the cup holders.

Jonah settled into the driver's seat, let out a deep sigh, and grasped the wheel in both hands.

"Uncle Jonah," I said, "have you ever seen something no one else did?"

Jonah turned his head. "You mean like on mushrooms. You should stay away from that stuff, Li. I know I'm not the best example but—"

"I don't do drugs. If you're an example of anything, it's what not to do." I snapped.

Jonah scrubbed his hand down his face.

"I'm sorry. I didn't mean that."

"It's okay." He didn't look at me. He turned the key in the ignition. The car sputtered before the engine was resuscitated back to life.

In fifteen minutes, I was home. The house seemed so vacant from the outside. When I walked inside, I hoped to hear Dad's rock music blaring from his studio downstairs. I wished I'd see Mom's purse and keys on the credenza. But the house didn't vibrate with life the way it used to.

I went upstairs to my parents' bedroom. Sometimes Sim liked to sleep on their bed. Poor thing, I was gone for two days, and she didn't have any food or water.

I stopped at the door. The bed was unmade. Dad's boots were on the floor, paint spattered on the worn leather. Mom's closet was open, stuffed with clothes. The silence and stillness chilled my bones. No sign of Sim. I eased the door closed as a sob rose in my chest.

I checked my room. My guitar was on the bed. Clothes were strewn all over the floor.

Downstairs, I stopped in the hallway. On the wall were photographs of me when I was little. A five-by-seven photograph of me, Mom, and Dad on our vacation to Nashville hung above the credenza. We stood in front of the Grand Ole Opry House next to the guitar big enough for the Jolly Green Giant to bang out a song. Dad wore his black Judas Priest t-shirt and charcoal jeans, a leather arm bangle around one wrist. His arm was across my shoulders. My hair was shorter, and I wore a t-shirt with cut-off sleeves. Behind me, stood Mom, her long, dark hair tied back. She wore a navy-blue dress. Mom showed her teeth when she smiled. Dad grinned in awe. I smirked. I grabbed the photograph from the wall.

Jonah's voice came from the kitchen. He was on the phone. He faced away from me. "Yeah, she's here now."

"Who are you talking to?" I asked.

Jonah turned around. Lids hid half his eyes as he looked down. A frown wrinkled the skin around the corners of his lips. He ended the call. "That was your caseworker."

"You called them?"

"Li, I'm sorry. You have to go with her."

"So they can put me in some stranger's house?"

"Li—"

I turned away from him and raced back up the stairs to my bedroom. I unzipped my backpack and turned it upside down. The books thudded onto the hardwood. I piled clothes from the floor and my closet into my backpack. Tears dripped onto the fabric as I packed. I placed the framed photograph on top of the pile of clothes in the backpack, but I thought better of it. I wanted the photo close to me.

My fingertips pulled back the tabs encasing the photo in the frame. The frame slipped out of my hands. Glass shattered.

The house shook, and bright light blinded me. I staggered back, tripped, and fell. Posters ripped from the walls. An angel knelt in the center of the room. His white wings were tucked behind him. He wore a hood of chainmail with a silver chest plate. The chainmail covered his arms and legs. Black gauntlets encased his hands. On his feet were boots tipped in steel. He lifted his head, and his eyes fastened on me.

I scrambled to my feet and raced into the hallway. The angel marched after me. *Zing!* He pulled a sword, silver with the image of wings fanned above the hilt. A round orb glowed with light on the pommel of the sword.

I still clenched the photo in my hand. I crinkled the picture as I grasped onto the photograph like a lifeline.

My back collided with the wall at the end of the hallway. The angel stalked towards me. He wanted to exterminate me like a cockroach.

You can make angels fall by touching them. Adriel's words echoed in my head. I hurled myself at the angel, hands raised. With a scream, I clawed at his face. I wanted to tear his eyes out. The angel screamed too.

He sidestepped me. I grabbed a handful of soft and downy feathers and fisted them in my hands as I fell to the floor.

I felt heat, hotter than the fire before Dad's car exploded. I backed away. The angel's wings burst into flames. His eyes grew dark like ink spilled into them. His face paled to sheet white, and embers floated around him.

I looked down at my hands. *The photo!* I searched the ground. Flames licked the edges of the photo. *No!* I stomped my foot down on the flames. I picked up the photo. The fire reduced the picture to half the original size. The faces of Mom and Dad were untouched, but the fire burned me out of the shot. I folded what was left of the picture and put it in my pocket.

The angel's shrieks stopped. The flames subsided, but they disintegrated the white feathers of his wings and left nothing but blackened bones like strokes of charcoal on paper. His black eyes stabbed me.

I darted around him and rushed back to my bedroom. Posters covered a window against the back wall. I slammed the door shut and locked it. I tore the posters from the window.

The door groaned. The wood splintered. I ducked behind my bed and got low to the floor.

The angel walked into the room. Soon, he would find me. What was the point of making angels fall if they could still come after me?

Light pierced my eyes. I stared across the room. A circle wavered in the center of the room. The circle was translucent like water. Another slant of light glowed from the edges of the wavering circle. Inside was a gray world like a circular painting except with more depth.

A woman appeared from the tear. Her golden blonde hair was in tight spiraled curls, and her forest green eyes enchanted me. She was dressed in a tight outfit as if she were going to yoga class. But from the look on the creature's face, she wasn't going to perform downward dog or the child's pose.

The creature froze. "You."

A smile curled upon her lips. With a powerful kick, she struck him in the chest. He staggered back. His sword clamored to the floor. A dagger flashed in her hand. She lunged at him. The creature was so focused on her dagger, he missed when her foot curled around his ankle. She pulled back hard. He collided with the floor.

The portal glowed behind her. Two men exited. One, light-skinned with charcoal black hair and the other dark-skinned with a curved sword at his hip. The two men approached the creature. Each grabbed an arm and hauled him to his feet.

The girl unhooked a set of manacles from her belt.

"I hope you won't make this difficult," said the dark-haired man. His eyes were as black as coals. He wore a zippered midnight blue shirt and fingerless black gloves. A thick, leather belt fastened around his waist. A sword encased in a sheath strung along the belt. Black pants ended in obsidian boots.

"Traitor," the creature hissed through his teeth.

The dark-skinned man wore black pants and a long-sleeve black shirt with padded leather shoulders. He withdrew his blade and tucked its sharp edge under the creature's chin. "I know you're in a lot of pain."

"What do you know about it?" The creature ground out.

"Nothing you're not finding out right now," said the black-eyed man.

The girl folded her arms. The manacles dangled from her hand. "You have a choice," she said. "You can walk on your own into this portal so we don't have to drag you, or I can let Kiran slice your throat open and send you to the Pit."

The cramp in my leg worsened. I stretched my leg. A dull thud echoed behind me. I cursed under my breath. My foot hit my dresser.

The girl looked around the room. "What was—"

The creature let out a howl and lunged back out of Kiran and the dark-eyed man's grasp. He staggered against the wall and flung himself onto the dark-eyed man.

"Nash!" the girl cried.

Nash and the angel rolled onto the ground. The angel was on top of him, his hands around Nash's neck. A dagger gleamed in Nash's hand. He drove the dagger into the angel's side.

Thick, black liquid bubbled from the angel's mouth and his hands loosened from around Nash's neck.

Nash rolled from under him and was behind him in one swift, graceful motion. Nash slashed the creature's throat. His chest heaved, and his blade dripped with the dark substance.

My hand flew to my mouth. Tears fell. My eyes ached.

Nash sighed and wiped the dark blood from his blade onto his black jacket. After a considerable amount of brackish blood spilled onto the floor, the angel became more and more translucent. I blinked. He disappeared.

Kiran knelt down and reached into his pocket. He pulled out a pinch of burned leaves, kissed them, and placed them where the angel's body had been.

"They're always so damn strong right after they fall," the girl said. "Tom should have warned us."

"He said it was a Cherub," said Kiran.

Nash shook his head. "He's a Dominion."

"You knew him?" asked the girl.

"No," said Nash. He lifted the angel's sword. "He mounted the orb of light to his sword."

"A traditionalist," said Kiran.

"Hardly," said Nash. "If he hadn't damned himself, I think we might have found him in the Pride Sector of the Angel District. Doesn't look like we'll need those." Nash motioned to the manacles clenched in the girl's hands.

Chirping echoed around the room as if birds sang from the rafters. The three looked at their wrists at what looked like watches with large, flat square faces.

"It's Tom. There's another one. Demon this time," said Nash, "near us. It's in a high school bathroom."

The girl disappeared into the portal followed by Kiran. Nash glanced around the room. His eyes fell on me. My breath caught. I saw something I wasn't supposed to see, would he—?

But he didn't approach me, didn't slash my throat like he did my attacker, he stepped through the portal and didn't look back.

four

"I!" Jonah's voice echoed down the hallway.

My legs wavered like plucked guitar strings as I rose from the side of the bed. I couldn't tell Jonah what I saw. He couldn't do anything about it. He would only worry about me.

Jonah's tall body stood in the frame of my door. "What were you doing down there?"

"Nothing." I slung my guitar strap across my shoulders and zipped my backpack. My hands still shook.

"I stepped outside," said Jonah. "I thought I heard a crash."

"I dropped a frame." I nodded toward the broken glass near the end of my bed. With my backpack in one hand and my guitar on my back, I approached the door.

Jonah moved out into the hallway, and I joined him, but I couldn't stay. I made my way to the stairs.

"Where are you going?" he asked.

"I won't stay in a foster home." I remembered what that was like. To be tossed from one foster family to the next because they couldn't handle the night terrors or the constant proclamations that I saw things other people didn't. The endless line of shrinks who told me the hallucinations were my way of dealing with trauma, what trauma, I couldn't remember. They wanted to put me on medication. They did put me on medication. "Take care of Sim for me."

Jonah grabbed my arm. "I can't let you leave. You're staying in this house."

I yanked my arm away. "You're not my dad."

Jonah's eyes widened as if I bit him. He frowned.

Hot tears erupted from my eyes as I tore down the steps. Three blocks away from the house, the sound of a motorcycle roared behind me.

Adriel pulled alongside me. "You went back home?" His voice burned me like a scraped knee.

"I needed to get my guitar."

"Is a guitar worth your life? You could have been attacked by one of Raphael's followers."

"I *was* attacked." My voice shook.

The gold melted again.

"An angel," I said. "I know what you meant. I watched him burn."

The angel, the blue eyes, and those beautiful, white wings. I touched those wings. They felt smooth, soft, and very *real*.

And when I touched them, they erupted into flames and turned to ash.

"He had a sword. I think he wanted to kill me." My voice sounded as if I tried to talk through wool.

"But he didn't." Adriel patted the back of the motorcycle. "We have to go."

"People came to get him," I continued. "They killed him, and he disappeared."

"Don't worry about that right now," said Adriel. "Raphael knows where you are. It won't be long before he gathers a group of his followers to come after you, and they'll be prepared." He handed me the helmet.

I gulped. He was right. Three streets from where I stood, an angel attacked me. I put the helmet on and got on the motorcycle. My guitar rested against my hip. I hugged my backpack between my chest and Adriel's back. I put the straps over my shoulders and gripped the grab rail. My eyes met Adriel's as he glanced over his shoulder. My body no longer shook.

In thirty minutes, we were back at the motel. I hadn't realized how close the sanctuary was to my house. My skin prickled. *What if Adriel was wrong? What if I wasn't safe here?*

I pushed the thought aside as we approached the motel room. I could taste the saltiness of my tears on my lips.

Adriel's hand touched the doorknob, and the handle glowed. The door popped open. He pulled me into the motel room and closed the door. He released me from his gloved hands.

NOT pulling the covers back, I sat on the motel room bed. The mattress felt odd as if filled with nothing but springs and air.

I flipped through the channels on the television. I settled on an infomercial that might put me to sleep. A dark-haired man with a grizzled beard spilled various liquids on a multitude of different surfaces and used one super absorbent rag to soak up the spills. The liquid was gone and, like magic, left no stain.

I wished my messes were as easy to clean up. I had no place else to go for the night. Jonah was determined to call family services on me. I had no money and no friends.

Jonah probably called the police and reported me as a runaway. They would look for me, and once they found me, I would be chucked into a foster home.

Adriel was outside. He said he would stand guard. I assumed he meant to keep others out, but maybe he meant to keep me in.

Adriel had wings and said he was an angel. He was real and so were the people who came to kill the angel I made fall. I had to believe it or admit I was crazy.

My sane mind told me the stress made the hallucinations seem more real. But Adriel could touch me, albeit with gloved hands, and he could restrain me. That was weird. He couldn't do that if he was a figment of my imagination, but maybe *he* wasn't. Sure, the wings and the talk of Archangels could be all in my head, but maybe he did bring me to this motel. He was a real person, without wings of course. But how could I explain the people dressed in black?

Adriel told me an Archangel was after me. Raphael. And I saw him crash onto my parents' car. He was the reason they were dead.

The whole thing was ludicrous to me, but on top of the free room, Adriel graced me with fast food, and I was hungry. I skipped lunch and spent the rest of the day with my eyes locked on the television screen. I couldn't recall what was on mere seconds after having watched it.

How did he get the fast food and the motel room? Angels weren't supposed to steal food or break into motels. He had money, a lot of it, but how did he get it? I couldn't imagine Adriel working a cash register at a grocery store or taking calls at a cubicle desk. Did he steal that money from someone? Angels were the good guys. They weren't supposed to murder either.

I scoffed down the entire meal in minutes and was glad Adriel wasn't in the room to see me chow down. Why did I feel the need to be polite to him? He kidnapped me. I couldn't believe everything he said. There had to be an explanation for all of this.

For argument's sake, let's say I wasn't crazy, and an Archangel was hell-bent on tracking me down. Still, Adriel was an angel too. Why would he have more of an alliance to me than to his own kind? If he was trying to save me, he could change his mind at any time. A layer of hate smoldered in his eyes. The hate was for me, for what I was. What *was* I?

Was it possible to be evil without knowing it? Was I like Damien from *The Omen*? I shook my head. Here I was considering whether I was the anti-Christ. I needed sleep.

I set the bedside alarm for 3 A.M. That's when I would sneak out the bathroom window and decide my next move. Whenever he was around, I had this odd trust in Adriel, but when he was away I could think without that distraction.

I was sixteen. I could get a job and maybe a fake I.D. But where would I sleep until my first paycheck?

My mind darted so much I couldn't sleep. I sat up and turned off the TV. I leaned my head against the headboard and closed my eyes.

Bright light danced behind my eyelids like I fell asleep sunbathing. The bed glided as if on wheels.

"Female, roughly fifteen, found at the scene of a crash. Right lateral bruising, could be internal bleeding. Possible concussion."

My eyes blinked open. People dressed in scrubs wheeled me on a bed down a bright, white hallway. I tried to turn my head. My neck was restrained. A woman's voice spoke, "You're with us, sweetheart. Hang in there. We'll get you fixed up real soon."

I squeezed my eyes shut, but the light still stung. Metal zinged. Were they going to cut me? My eyelids shot open.

Darkness receded. A bright light hovered above me. Out of that light came Raphael. His bright blue eyes stabbed me in the heart as his staff came down.

I jolted up from bed and stifled the scream with my hands. Darkness veiled me in its protection, and the only light came from the television that droned an infomercial about knives. My chest rose and fell in rapid breaths. I grabbed the remote from the bedside table and flicked off the TV. The room was bathed in silence. I put my head in my hands.

Meow! I glanced around the room. A muffled *tap*, *tap* brought me to my feet. I followed the sound. *Was I hearing things now?* Could I trust anything I saw or heard?

My bare feet swept across the nylon carpet to the bathroom where the sound was louder. My head darted in the direction of the sound. Above the toilet was a small window, the window I planned to sneak out of when I made my escape.

A cat tapped the window with her paw.

I slid the window open, and the cat jumped into my arms. I stroked her fur.

"Sim?"

I looked for any familiar features in the moonlight. She had dark gray fur and unique black markings.

"How did you get here?"

I hugged her to my chest and glanced out the window. On the pavement was a line of white. The line was broken and granules, like salt or sugar, streaked across the ground.

I furrowed my brow and tried to see where the curved line ended. The line coiled around the side of the building.

I brought Sim to the bed, settled down next to her, and pet down the length of her back.

"You shouldn't have come here," I said. "It'll be hard enough to take care of myself."

I found Sim outside our house when she was a kitten. After I fed her for weeks, Mom allowed me to let her inside.

I scratched behind her ear, and she purred.

"We'll have to leave soon," I said. "It's just you and me now."

THE alarm went off. I made sure to keep the volume low so Adriel couldn't hear the noise from the outside.

I turned off the alarm, sat up in bed, and rubbed my eyes.

I stretched my arms over my head but stopped mid-stretch when my eyes caught an outline in the darkness.

Someone sat, in the corner of the room, in the worn, motel armchair. I blinked and looked again. The whites of his eyes glowed in the dark. A slant of angled light streamed in front of him from the bathroom window. The dim glow graced the black fabric of his pants. He wore a black shirt and a black suit. His tie was a trail of crimson. The shadows veiled his face.

"Quite a night we're having," he said with the shadow of contempt in his voice.

I folded my legs up to my chest. "Who are you? What are you doing here?"

"You can call me Bob." His body folded into the chair like a tarantula in a matchbox.

I peered through the darkness. No semblance of wings.

"Are you an angel too?" I said with an edge to my voice.

"I'm no angel, sweetheart." He leaned forward in his chair. His face entered the stream of light. His skin was orange like he had a bad experience with sunless tanning. His eyes were black. The pupils seemed too big. His thin lips were low on his face. His dark hair was slicked back. He looked forty, maybe forty-five.

His hands were clasped in front of him like he was conducting a business meeting. "The difference between me and the angels is that I don't want to kill you."

I narrowed my eyes. He said he didn't want to kill me, but his tone made me feel like that's *exactly* what he wanted to do.

I raised my eyebrow. "Adriel brought me here to help me." I wasn't sure if that was true, but this man might know something, and I wanted to know what he knew.

"Adriel? The young Seraph standing in the parking lot? You think he could stop Raphael?" He stared at me. "I judge by your lack of surprise that you know about Raphael. Even if that little angel could stand a chance against one of the oldest Archangels in existence, why would he? You know one angel is after you, maybe Adriel pulled you away from the rescue party. Maybe he plans to deliver you to Raphael himself and receive a reward. You don't know anything about him."

"I don't know anything about you either."

"You can see I don't have wings, can't you?" He glanced behind both his shoulders in turn.

"That doesn't mean that you're on my side." I crossed my arms.

"No, I guess not. You'll have to decide." He snapped his fingers, and a large circle glowed alongside him like a tear in the space. A ripple fizzled like lightning and surrounded the circle. Inside was a gray scene, a road and buildings in the distance.

"My boss sent me to rescue you," said Bob. "Don't make me go home empty handed. It could mean the Pit for me."

I stared into the hole as if the opening was a mouth that could swallow me. The tear looked like the one that the people in black climbed through. They saved me from that angel, unintentionally, but one of them let me live despite what I saw.

Sim padded across the bed. Her black and gray form glided in front of me. I reached out for her, but before I could grasp her, her long, sleek body jumped into the tear. She looked out to me from across the gray street.

Bob pressed the fingers of one hand to his thumb in rapid secession as if he played a flute. "Last chance, sweetheart."

five

I climbed through the bright portal. My stomach lurched, and my head swam. A force pulled at me like the momentum that jerks you when riding bumper cars.

My guitar slung across my back, I clenched my backpack. A rush of air, scented like the breeze before the rain, hit me. I looked at the sky. The clouds were layers of gray. I couldn't find the sun. Light came from the ground in the distance. The glow peered between the buildings and gave the whole street a dreamlike quality.

The grimy motel was replaced by a five-star hotel, and all the buildings looked like modern art. One jutted out from the ground like a skyscraper. The building was a mix of grays, whites, and blacks. Another looked like a series of clean, smooth, white and gray boxes stacked on top of each other with floor to ceiling windows along one entire side of the building.

No trash littered the street. No graffiti ran alongside the buildings. Everything looked clean, crisp, and slate gray.

Sim rubbed against my legs, and I stooped to pick her up.

The roar of an engine reared up behind me. I turned around, and Bob sat in a black convertible with the top down. He winked at me.

"Get in," he said. "Unless you want to walk."

The portal disappeared like the zipper on a jacket. The space was unblemished by the rip. The smooth space looked as if the wound could never be reopened.

"Am I...trapped here?" I asked.

"We're all trapped here, sweetheart," Bob said.

That didn't make much sense. After all, how could Bob be trapped if he could make portals appear and disappear at will?

Bob's suit was darker. The suit turned from charcoal black to obsidian. His tie was a bloodier shade of red.

He flashed straight, white teeth. A shiny gold watch wrapped around his wrist.

He looked like a well-groomed businessman, but something felt...*sinister* about him. At least he didn't have wings.

He was either part of my least crazy subconscious, or this was real. This *felt* real.

I pulled open the passenger side door and got in with Sim. What choice did I have? The street was familiar, settled right under the bypass, but the buildings were foreign to me. I wouldn't know where I was going.

The car picked up speed and careened around the corner. Bob jabbed the pedal, and the car jolted forward.

I dug my nails into the seat. Where did this guy learn to drive?

We rounded a corner.

"Where are you taking me?" I yelled as the car sped down the street.

"Someplace much better than that ratty, old motel. Nash won't mind."

Nash, I heard that name before. He was one of the men who crawled through a portal into my bedroom. He inadvertently saved my life, and he killed someone else to do that.

"Who's Nash?"

"He's the guy who owns *this* place." The wheels screeched as we came to a halt in front of a mansion. A literal mansion. The place was lined with gray stone and plaster. It rose at least thirty feet in the air with plenty of large windows along the front face. The brick patio led to a set of stone steps. Lights glowed inside the building.

Bob stepped out of the car, and I followed. He was very tall, at least six foot five maybe taller. He towered over me and the car.

Bob opened the door to the mansion. Who keeps a place like this unlocked?

I walked in after Bob. The walls were alabaster. Mirrors hung on the walls, and the illusion made the place seem larger. A marble staircase rose from the front entrance.

Bob walked up the stairs and gestured for me to follow.

"Why are we going upstairs?" I asked.

"So, I can show you to your room."

"*My* room?"

"You woke up pretty early," said Bob. "It's going to be a few more hours till morning."

"Wait, but what time is it?" I asked.

"3:18," he said, but he didn't look down at his watch or cellphone.

"But it's light outside. Well, sort of."

"Overcast." Bob said. "It's always like that here."

He had to be exaggerating. The weather had to change sometimes.

"Where's here?" I asked.

"Sheol," said Bob.

I narrowed my eyes. "Where is that from New Orleans?"

"South." Bob grinned. "Sheol is always south."

I shook my head and waited for a white rabbit with a pocket watch to scurry around a corner.

"Is Nash home?" I asked.

"Why? Do you want to meet him?"

Do I want to meet the guy whose house I was staying the night in? "Yes," I said. "I don't want to wake him, but, I mean, I am in his house. Are you going to tell him?"

Bob laughed. "He knows who you are."

How was that possible? I just met Bob. Nash did see me before he entered that portal, but it's not like I stepped up and introduced myself.

Bob stopped at a large frosted glass door and slid it open. The room was hospital white. The bed in the center rested on a glass platform that made the mattress look like it hovered.

"You should get comfortable," said Bob. "It won't be long before Nash finds out you're here." He said that like I was a mouse, and Nash was a cat. Like he wanted to hunt me down once he knew I was in his house.

Bob closed the door behind him as he walked back out into the hallway. His footsteps became distant.

I slumped onto the bed with Sim still in my arms. I sighed.

I tried to think of something, anything that could explain all of this. I couldn't be crazy. Crazy people don't know they're crazy.

I shook my head. I pinched myself a thousand times since I met Adriel, and I didn't wake up.

I needed to go through with this, find out why a psycho angel was after me and go home, back to reality. But the death of my parents shattered my reality. What I returned to wouldn't be the home I knew.

Sim bounced to the floor. I laid on the bed. The mattress was firm, and the sheets were cool to the touch.

My thoughts pulled sleep from me until exhaustion extinguished them.

WHEN I woke, the light in the room glowed with the same intensity as the night before despite the large window. I sat up and looked outside. Bob wasn't joking. The sky's color did not change nor was the street wet with rain.

I got goose bumps as I left the warmth of the bed.

Two smaller doors of frosted glass stood in the room besides the door that led out to the hallway. I padded across the cold floor to the door across from the bed.

Behind the door was a closet filled with clothes that hung on either side and a large mirror on the back wall. Recessed lights brightened every inch of the room. A large white chest of drawers was set in the center.

I pulled a garnet red dress from the closet rod. The fabric touched the floor. I frowned and hung the dress back up.

As I browsed through the clothing, I felt like more of an intruder.

Whose room was this?

I left the closet and walked to the door across from the other side of the bed.

Holy shit!

A walk-in shower was built into one corner of the room. Curved glass surrounded the shower. Alongside the shower was a large marble platform with a small step leading up to it. Set into the center of the marble platform was a bathtub and hollowed out into the wall across from the tub was a built-in fireplace. Across from all this was a marble countertop and sink, above which was a wall of mirrors that stretched from one end of the bathroom to the other.

I didn't belong here.

I turned the silver handle on the sink and wet my face in the basin. The water ran cool and clear and felt soothing.

I washed my face with a bar of hard soap that didn't have a scent, dried my face on a white towel, and peered at my reflection. My hair was in tangles. The dyed ends were wet from falling into the sink. My clothes were wrinkled. A bruise purpled along my jawline, and my bottom lip was split.

I pulled open the drawer, and inside was a brush and comb. I ran the brush through my hair until the knots were out.

I reached into my pocket and pulled out the burnt picture of my parents. My face tensed into a frown and lips quivered. The golden locket Jonah had given me hung around my neck. I searched the drawers and found a pair of cuticle scissors. I cut a heart around my Mom and Dad's faces. I had to trim them a few times before they fit inside the locket. Their photographs were side by side nestled within two hearts.

I wore the same clothes from three days ago. They smelled of sweat and blood. I unzipped my backpack and pulled out a t-shirt and cutoffs. They were wrinkled because I tossed them, unfolded, into the bag. I took off my old clothes and put on the new ones.

I thought I should take a shower, but felt weird about it. I'd never been in a house this nice and pristine. I was sure whatever I did would leave a mark. I felt carsick.

I smoothed out my shirt as best as I could. As I ran my hands over my stomach, it rumbled. I'd have to find food for me and Sim. The prospects of that were better than if I had snuck through the motel window.

I didn't like roaming around the house of a guy I never met, but I was eager to find the kitchen. Sooner or later, he would know I was in his house. I hoped he didn't think I was an intruder. Didn't Bob say that Nash knew me? Did he mean my name or what I looked like too? Did he know I was the girl he saw after he murdered that angel?

I made a terrible detective. I couldn't get the right answers if I didn't ask the right questions. I should have told Bob what I knew about Nash. He might have given me more information, like why Nash jumped through portals and killed angels.

I opened the door and tiptoed out of the room. The hallway was empty. Recessed lights bathed the hall in a sun-like glow, and the air smelled clean and sterile like a clinic. Sim followed me.

"No, Sim, you stay." I lifted her from the ground and placed her back in the room before I slid the door shut.

My steps echoed like footfalls in a museum. I bit my lip and squeezed my eyes shut. *Should I take off my shoes?*

I crept down the marble stairs to the foyer. To my right was the living room. To my left was a hallway. I wandered down the hall and stopped.

An entrance opened to the kitchen. White cupboards ran along the walls near the ceiling. Ivory counters settled above black cabinets along the wall and on the island. A stainless-steel refrigerator stood level with the upper cabinets. A coffee pot sat on the counter next to the sink. Light glowed from an oval, white light fixture hanging from the ceiling and from beneath the island.

I pulled open the fridge and peered inside. On the shelves were vegetables, jars of jam, a pitcher of water, plum colored juice, and a bowl of peaches.

I looked through the cabinets until I found an array of glasses and pulled one down from the shelf. I poured a glass of the purplish juice and drank it in a few gulps. The juice was sweet and sour.

I took the cup from my lips when someone appeared through the bottom of the glass.

Nash stood by the coffee pot. He pulled a jar down from the top shelf. He looked no older than twenty. He was tall with charcoal black hair, alarming against his pale skin. His eyes were so dark I couldn't distinguish the pupils from the irises. He wore a thin, sleeveless t-shirt and boxer-shorts.

My eyes hit the floor. "Sorry. Bob said…"

"Good morning." He scooped coffee beans out of the jar. He didn't seem to recognize me although he only glanced at me.

"You must be Nash," I said.

"That's right." He didn't turn to look at me. He lifted the top of the coffee machine and filled the chamber with the coffee beans.

I must have embarrassed him. Did he expect me to leave?

The muscles of his back moved beneath the barely-there t-shirt.

"You hungry?" He still didn't look at me.

"Yeah, I guess."

"Tofu scramble okay?"

"Um, you don't have to cook for me."

"Okay. I thought you might be hungry."

"I am," I said.

"Then how about the scramble?" He turned around and gave me a tight smile.

"Sure." Truth was I never had tofu. Mom used to make me scrambled eggs. She made the best scrambled eggs.

"You can wait in the dining room. It shouldn't take long."

"Where's the dining room?"

Nash pointed to the frosted door on the opposite wall.

I took my glass and ducked out, happy to leave the tension behind me. A marble table was in the center of the dining room. Ten gray, cushioned chairs surrounded the table. Two paintings hung side by side on the wall. One painting was gray with white lines scratched into the canvas. The other was cream-colored with charcoal lines in a mess of spirals.

Dad's paintings showed dark imagery, but they had meaning. I wondered what those paintings meant.

I pulled my cellphone out of my pocket. I should call Jonah. I couldn't tell him where I was. I wasn't sure where I was. But I wanted to let him know I was okay.

The screen lit up. No service. I walked around the room. Still, no service. Weird. Thirty percent battery charge. I turned the phone off and stowed it in my pocket.

NASH walked into the dining room with my breakfast. He had changed into a white collared shirt and dark pants. He left the shirt untucked.

He set my plate down in front of me. The tofu scramble looked like scrambled eggs without the yolks.

Nash stood against the opposite wall and sipped his coffee. His eyes were pointed at the opposite wall where the paintings hung. Did he know the meaning behind those dark squiggles and those sharp, white lines?

The texture of the tofu was spongy. The flavor was earthy, nutty, and spicy. The mushrooms and peppers gave it pops of color. As I chewed, I tried not to scoff the food down. My fork hit the plate with a loud clang. I cringed.

I glanced up, but Nash's eyes still focused on the opposite wall.

I hated to ask, but I needed to get Sim something to eat too. "Um...do you have any tuna fish...it's for my cat."

"Sorry. No." Nash sipped his coffee.

"Do you have any other meat or fish or anything?"

"I don't have any of that here."

That's a little odd. Maybe he was vegetarian.

"Okay," I said. "Is there a store nearby?"

"I'll get you some this afternoon." He took another sip of his coffee. "First, I'll have to bring you into town. The boss wants to see you."

NASH climbed into the driver seat of a sleek red car. A tiny silver horse galloped on the grill. I settled down into the passenger's seat. By Nash's attitude back at the house, I guessed this ride would be painfully silent.

Nash said we were going to see his boss, but he made no effort to tuck his white button-down shirt into his pants. Bob dressed in a fitted black suit and red tie. Did they work for the same guy? And why was this guy interested in keeping me safe from an Archangel?

At least, no one I'd met since Adriel had wings. That was a plus on my reality meter.

The sky was still the same dull gray. The air still smelled like it does right before a rainstorm, and I expected a downpour.

Nash pulled the car out of the driveway and floored it down the street. I braced myself on the dashboard as he continued to zip down the road like he drove for NASCAR. Did everyone in this place drive like a freaking maniac?

The images outside began to blur, and I got dizzy. I thought I might throw up. I grabbed my stomach as the car lurched to a stop.

Nash got out of the car. I stayed in my seat and covered my mouth as I clenched my stomach. Nash's face appeared in the window. He frowned. Was that concern?

He opened the door for me, and I stepped out of the car. My legs shook like cymbals hit with a drumstick. Nash held my elbow to steady me. His touch was warm. The heat seeped beneath the sleeve of my shirt.

We stopped outside a skyscraper that was several stories high like a corporate building. Clouds hid the top of the structure. The glass door slid open. A secretary sat behind a white desk that wrapped around in a semi-circle. Her round, clear face held a tight smile that spread from ear to ear and showed all her teeth. The wide smile made her cheekbones rise, and her eyes crinkle to slits.

"Good morning," she said. "You must be here for your 10:00 A.M. appointment, you can wait in room 1006."

Nash nodded to her as we headed for the elevator. Nash jabbed a button and waited with his hands in his pockets.

I glanced at the button that still glowed: 1000. *One thousand floors? That must be a joke.*

My body jolted as the elevator rose. The sickening feeling festered in my stomach as the elevator lurched upwards. I could feel my breakfast rising in my throat.

The doors opened to a wall of floor to ceiling windows. I walked to the windows and glanced down. I couldn't see the cars below. Clouds obscured my vision. The sky was dark like it was 10:00 P.M. instead of 10:00 A.M. The dark clouds swallowed the building.

I was dizzy. I wasn't afraid of heights, but this was different. When Felicia and I were friends, her parents brought us to Six

Flags. Felicia wanted to ride the highest rollercoaster but not unless I rode with her. I never rode a rollercoaster in my life, and I screamed every time the cars dropped, but that didn't make me as sick as when I stood above the clouds.

A warm hand touched my shoulder. I jumped.

"Are you afraid?" Nash asked.

I felt my head nod involuntarily while I said, "No."

He smiled. "This way."

I followed him and scratched the back of my hand as I read the numbers on each door: 1014, 1012, 1010, 1008....

Nash pushed open the door to room 1006. In the room was a white leather sofa across from two black armchairs and a plush rug against the hard marble floor. On a glass coffee table, between the sofa and chairs, rested a wilted lily in a ceramic pot.

"Have a seat," said Nash.

I turned to sit and was startled by a lady in the corner. She wore a white skirt suit and had the same creepy smile as the secretary downstairs.

She glided forward and stopped in front of us. "Can I get you anything?"

"Coffee," said Nash.

Second coffee today. Long night, buddy?

She turned her head and smiled at me.

"Nothing for me, thanks." I needed water. My mouth was drier than a raisin. But I didn't want that strange woman to get it for me.

The woman turned on her heel and left the room. She walked so straight-backed and with such perfect spacing between each step, she couldn't be real. She was like a creepy mannequin brought to life.

After she left, I realized I was hovering above the sofa. I sat down. Nash sat on the other end of the sofa with one arm stretched across the back while the other lay on the armrest.

His hand was inches from my face as his arm closed the distance between us.

My hands were clasped in my lap. My eyes looked down at them. I crossed and uncrossed my legs. Neither pose was comfortable for long. I thought I would break the silence, when the door opened. The secretary walked in with Nash's coffee.

He accepted the cup from her and took one long sip.

The woman retired to the same corner of the room and turned away from us. I squinted at her, but I was glad I couldn't see her face. Her smile might give me nightmares.

The door opened again. Bob strode in, dressed in the same black suit and red tie. He glanced at me and smiled. He held the door open for someone.

Her face was pale and thin with burgundy red lipstick. She wore a fitted, black pantsuit with red cuffs and tall red heels, not that she needed them as her head was an inch from the doorframe.

But what made my eyes go wide and my hands start to sweat, wasn't her height or the rail thinness of her body, but what followed.

As her full form strolled through the doorway, from her back was a set of blackened bones that came up in two angled arches above each shoulder and sank down to thin points near the middle of her calves. They were like wings that lost all their feathers. They were like the wings of the angel I touched.

Bob sat in one of the black chairs across from the sofa while the tall woman stood behind the chair's twin. Her long fingers curled upon the soft leather of the chair's back. Each nail was long and black like a talon.

Run! But I could feel those claws ripping through my body if I made any move toward the door. I glanced over at Nash, but he sipped his coffee and lifted the mug with steady hands.

Bob crossed his legs and folded his hands in his lap. He smiled at me like I was the entertainment.

My eyes darted back to the long nails and up to the woman's face. Her thin lips curled into a smile.

"Have my boys been treating you well?" she asked.

I nodded without thinking. I wanted to ask a hundred questions, but I couldn't will myself to speak.

"I have a few things I need to explain to you first, darling. Then, you can talk, okay?"

I nodded again without meaning to.

"You're being hunted by an Archangel, honey. Well, you probably knew that part. His name is Raphael, and he has an agenda, you see. He doesn't want to kill you. He wants to *use* you. He wants to use you to close the gates of Heaven forever. And I can't have that. Alright, we've got that out of the way."

My voice came back.

My eyes swept from her pale face, and the arched bones rose above her shoulders. She was the boss in this place, this place that was separate from the world. Why hadn't I seen it sooner?

One question burned me, one I wasn't sure I wanted the answer to.

"Are you the Devil?"

"Name's Lucifer, honey. And no, you can't call me Lucy."

I gulped. "Am I...in Hell?"

"I hate that word," said Lucifer. "We call it Sheol. Still Hell, but it doesn't have the same bite."

Either way, I was in Hell. *The* Hell. I don't care what the Devil calls it. Did I die? Was Bob the Grim Reaper?

"Am I dead?"

"No," said Lucifer. "Unfortunately, killing you might not solve my problem. You could still be of use to Raphael."

"Why is Raphael after me? I don't understand. How could he use *me*?"

"Because you can kill angels, my dear. Well, not literally. No one can *kill* an angel. But you can make them fall from grace."

Adriel told me the same. But I assumed Raphael wanted me dead because of what I could do, not that he wanted to use me.

"But why would Raphael want to close the gates of Heaven?" I asked.

"Because he's jealous. He doesn't want you or your kind in Heaven. All those souls to look after, to take care of. You would be his weapon against the angels who resist. Not all the angels agree with Raphael. They still think they are upholding God's will although most of them have never seen Him."

I closed my eyes. I pinched my arm once, twice, but I was still met with Lucifer's black eyes. "Why do you care? If the gates of Heaven are closed, there's only one other place for souls to go."

"Precisely," said Lucifer. "We're overcrowded as it is. I'll have to throw more souls into the Pit."

Bob cringed.

"Besides," she said. "I'm very...particular about the souls I take. Some of course, have to come here, but I like to be selective."

"So, I can't leave."

"Not unless you want to be Raphael's tool. But I do have a proposition for you." Lucifer drummed her fingers against the front of the chair. "I want you to make Raphael and all his followers fall."

My mind raced. This was not the side I wanted to be on. I wasn't religious, but everyone knows that the Devil is the bad guy...or *girl*. "Why should I do that for you?"

"You're damned. Your soul is on my list. If you want it back, you'll play along."

On her list? I was destined for Hell. How was that possible? "I don't understand."

"Bob, show her the paperwork."

Bob opened the folder in his lap and passed a sheet of paper over to me. The document was in a language I couldn't understand, and the bottom was stained in blood.

"I can't read this."

"Oh, sorry, sweetheart." Bob waved his hand over the paper, and the letters morphed into English.

I skimmed over the contents.

I remembered all those times I clicked agree before reading the terms and conditions. Did I agree to sell my soul every time I downloaded a new app to my phone?

"That smear on the bottom, that's the signature," Lucifer said. "We do them in blood now. Far less tricky."

"I don't remember signing anything," I said. "Not in writing or in blood."

"You didn't," said Lucifer. "Your mother did the honors before you were born."

I narrowed my eyes. My mother sold my soul to the Devil?

www.ingramcontent.com/pod-product-compliance
Lightning Source LLC
Chambersburg PA
CBHW031318170626
46807CB00002B/461